Don't lose you...

He had to make sure she was hemodynamic for transportation to a hospital. Amazing that she'd survived the night. How many times had they found people out here in the bush who hadn't survived?

"I need you to tell me where you hurt the most." Cole began looking in her ears, mouth, nose, and then he pressed on her stomach to check for internal bleeding. She seemed okay. "Where else do you hurt, Sashi? Can you move your fingers for me?"

She looked at him with serious eyes. "What if I can never dance again?"

"Sashi, never stop believing in miracles. You are alive, miracle number one."

Dear Reader,

Cole's story is one that I have longed to tell since he appeared into the novella "A Daughter's Discovery" from *A Mother's Wedding Day* (American Romance #1302). I imagined his character as an incredibly sexy doctor with a tortured past he couldn't seem to outrun.

Writing this story was an amazing adventure. I wanted Cole to find true love, but his path to Sashi Hansen is one full of pain and soul searching. In order for him to help Sashi overcome a horrific attack from a bear, he has to deal with the loss of his brother as he fights for her love.

I hope you enjoy this book. It's been a personal journey for not just my hero and heroine, but for me as well.

Ciao,

Dominique

The Alaskan Rescue

DOMINIQUE BURTON

HARLEQUIN® AMERICAN ROMANCE®

Recycling programs
for this product may
not exist in your area.

ISBN-13: 978-0-373-75444-1

THE ALASKAN RESCUE

Copyright © 2013 by Dominique Burton

All rights reserved. Except for use in any review, the reproduction or utilization of this work in whole or in part in any form by any electronic, mechanical or other means, now known or hereafter invented, including xerography, photocopying and recording, or in any information storage or retrieval system, is forbidden without the written permission of the publisher, Harlequin Enterprises Limited, 225 Duncan Mill Road, Don Mills, Ontario M3B 3K9, Canada.

This is a work of fiction. Names, characters, places and incidents are either the product of the author's imagination or are used fictitiously, and any resemblance to actual persons, living or dead, business establishments, events or locales is entirely coincidental.

This edition published by arrangement with Harlequin Books S.A.

For questions and comments about the quality of this book, please contact us at CustomerService@Harlequin.com.

® and TM are trademarks of Harlequin Enterprises Limited or its corporate affiliates. Trademarks indicated with ® are registered in the United States Patent and Trademark Office, the Canadian Trade Marks Office and in other countries.

Printed in U.S.A.

www.Harlequin.com

ABOUT THE AUTHOR

As a young girl with three brothers and a writer for a mother, Dominique Burton lived in the imaginary world of books such as *Anne of Green Gables* and movies starring Indiana Jones. Much of the time, she would write and act out her own stories with Harrison Ford as the hero. Not too shabby for a seven-year-old! Dominique loves Europe, and at the age of twenty, got the wild notion to buy an around-the-world, one-way plane ticket. For six months, she circled the globe alone, studying Italian, learning about other cultures, scuba diving and having a blast. She graduated from the University of Utah with a bachelor's degree in history. She now lives in South Jordan, Utah, with her husband, two children and three stepchildren, all of whom she dearly loves. If she's not writing or reading, she's out running. A few years ago, Dominique had the privilege of running the Boston Marathon. To learn more, go to www.dominiqueburton.com.

Books by Dominique Burton

HARLEQUIN AMERICAN ROMANCE

1302—A MOTHER'S WEDDING DAY
   "A Daughter's Discovery"
1376—THE FIREFIGHTER'S CINDERELLA

The Alaskan Rescue was a challenging book to write. The heroine's bear attack and the hero's past guilt of losing a loved one developed into an intricate story line. Internet research alone didn't have all the answers.

First of all I want to thank my editor, Kathleen Scheibling, for giving me the chance to write a book that explored these topics.

I want to thank Ben Walker, a real ranger of the Tongass National Forest. He helped me to understand black bears, from their size to their natural aptitudes.

My love and appreciation goes to Dr. Stephanie C. Gardner, M.D., a dear old friend who explained the ABCs of Emergency Medicine. (Love you!) My thanks goes out to my buddy, Dr. Ben Curtis, M.D., who took time out of his schedule to explain orthopedic injuries and how physical therapy helps treat them.

One of the main themes of the story is overcoming survivor's guilt. Plunging into this was more difficult than I had anticipated. This book could never have been as dramatic if Dr. Michael A. Kalm, M.D.—a man who has been one of the greatest influences in my life—hadn't shared his wisdom.

I know there have been many more people who have influenced this story. I want the reader to know that I take full responsibility for any errors or inconsistencies. My hope is that all who read this book will take away a little of the genius of the above individuals who made such a valuable contribution to my book.

Chapter One

Dr. Cole Stevens looked out the window of his pontoon Cessna, trying to get a better look at Marshall's Fishing Lodge and Resort. The large upscale property, nestled in a cove on the Inside Passage of southeast Alaska, was set against the emerald rain forest of the gentle hills of Prince of Wales Island.

Because he was a nature lover at heart, Cole did his best never to take the splendor of the world he lived in for granted. As a bush doctor he felt blessed to have a job he loved. He didn't always know where his day would take him. Sometimes he would be at the hospital. Other times he'd be helping with search-and-rescue out in the middle of nowhere.

On this late August day he was here to find out what type of illness had struck a group of fishermen from Kansas who were staying at Marshall's. As Cole expertly set his Cessna down on the choppy water and steered it toward the dock, he thought about Frank Marshall and his family's shabby treatment of employees and the people who lived on the island.

A local, Cole was well aware that the Marshall family had a hard time keeping employees, even though the pay was excellent. It took a tough person to handle the brutal hours and the family's habit of treating staff like indentured servants. But if you needed the money, he guessed it was worth it.

This got him thinking about the conversation he'd had earlier in the day with his best friend— Jake Powell, the chief ranger of the Tongass National Forest. Jake had been visiting Ketchikan where Cole lived, and had taken him out to lunch, something that rarely happened these days. Normally if Cole wanted to see his buddy, he had to fly from Prince of Wales Island to the small town of Craig, Alaska, to visit him and his family.

"I've got about fifteen minutes for lunch," he told Jake.

"Since when?" Jake took a swallow of beer and scowled at Cole. "Come on. We've had this lunch planned for weeks."

"Nature of my job." Cole hurriedly ate his sandwich. "I've got to fly up to Marshall's and take care of some sick people."

"Why don't you tell Frank Marshall to take a long hike on a short dock?" Jake said. "The Marshalls have ruined the sport of fishing with that new technology, and you know it!"

"Not really. I'm a terrible fisherman." Cole took

a sip of his soda. "And all the technology in the world wouldn't make *me* a better one."

Jake set his beer down and grinned at his friend. "Yes, you *are* a terrible fisherman. Remind me again why we're friends."

"Beats me. Yet you're here paying for lunch."

Jake straightened. "Now why is that? You're the rich doctor. You should be paying."

Cole shook his head. "Nope. You lost your bet. That last rescue we did—I said it would take three days to get out, and you said two, but I was right. Three horrible days."

"I need another beer." Jake swallowed the remains of the first, then called out to the waitress. "I hated that rescue. That guy—" he shook his head in disgust "—total jerk."

Cole agreed. "Almost worse than Frank Marshall. What was his name? Brek?"

"Brekker. Brekker Harris from Colorado." Jake imitated the man's voice.

Cole burst out laughing. "The guy still thought he was some mountain man even though we had to carry him out of the bush on foot."

"I don't know how you handle dealing with Old Man Marshall as much as you do."

"This trip has nothing to do with him. It's about the lodge guests who are sick at his place." Cole studied his friend. "Tell me—has Freddy been up to his old tricks lately?"

"Hey, are you asking me for info after you've

only given me a few minutes of your precious time?" Jake's face broke into a grin again. "I'm not talking. It's part of my job."

Cole finished his sandwich with one last bite. "Come on."

Jake shook his head. "My lips are sealed."

"Come *on*—" Cole threw his hands in the air and leaned back, cocking his head at Jake. "Did Freddy bring girls up from the lower forty-eight? He's done it before."

"You're killing me, Cole. Okay. But this stays between you and me."

Cole ran a hand through his short sandy hair. "Oh yeah, because I'm gonna gossip like a school girl. You know me better than that, Jake." He leaned forward. "I'm waiting."

Jake sighed. "Well, I just happened to do a random check on some of the Marshall boats while Freddy was out fishing. Every boat had fish catches over the limit. I issued a lot of citations that day."

"That's nothing new. Go on. What else?"

"Rumor has it that Freddy, who's been attending college in Washington, D.C., brought four women there to work this summer at the resort."

"And?" Cole began to drum his fingers on the table.

Jake leaned in closer. "All the women thought Freddy was in love with them. Apparently they each thought he'd brought her home to meet Daddy and propose. It's been a really nasty summer."

"Instead, he brought them home to work like slaves for his father," Cole said flatly.

"You got it."

"Typical Freddy." Cole finished his soda. "Okay, pal, gotta go."

It had been good to see Jake. While Cole was still remembering their conversation, the door of his plane was opened before he had completely shut the engine down. It brought Cole back to the present in a hurry.

"Good to see you, Doc."

"You, too, Randy. I didn't know you were working here now."

"Had to. The cannery let me go. Now Shirley is pregnant with our third and ain't feelin' well. Fred Marshall made me an offer I couldn't refuse."

"What's the catch?" Cole knew there had to be one. Randy looked exhausted.

"I get a day off every other week."

"How many hours a day are you working?"

"Eighteen. But this talk is between you and me, right? Doctor patient confidentiality and all."

Aghast at Randy's working conditions, Cole reached into the rear of the plane to grab his bag and a few supplies in case he needed to administer meds. When he turned back, he was calm enough to talk to Randy and stay out of his business. "Yes, Randy. What you say to me is confidential. You're a good man and father. Just…take care of yourself."

"I will."

With that Cole climbed out of the plane, knowing Randy would keep an eye on things. He always found it difficult to come to such a stunning place where the rich and famous played, and see firsthand how much the staff, hired for the wealthy guests' care and comfort, suffered. Now he needed to find Frank.

Cole walked into the main lodge. A large wooden structure, it had lacquered beams that reached at least thirty feet high. The lobby was centered by a rock fireplace rising to the roof. It took your breath away.

Today it was ablaze, creating a cozy atmosphere. For the visitors' convenience, leather couches, with throws of various animal furs, were placed here and there, while the walls were covered with stuffed trophy fish, animal heads and incredible photographs of Alaska.

In the back of each alcove, where either a concierge or bellhop was stationed, was a mounted bear or mountain goat. A true fisherman's and hunter's paradise. Cole's mind, however, was on the sick people. He went to the front desk, behind which stood a tall brunette. She smiled at him.

"Welcome to Marshall's," she said. "I'm Kendra. How may I assist you?"

"I'm Dr. Cole Stevens. Frank Marshall called me earlier to fly out and check on some guests who are ill."

She nodded. "We've been waiting for you. Mr. Marshall has been very worried. If you'll follow me, I'll take you to him."

IT WAS OVER AN HOUR LATER when Frank Marshall finally caught up with Cole.

"How did it go with the patients?"

Cole eyed the man who'd fed a lie to him before paying him to fly out here. Frank was a tall, handsome, charismatic man in his mid-sixties. Yet Cole knew he could turn into a viper if things didn't go the way he wanted. His son, Freddy, was just as bad. "Luckily for you things are all right."

"That's great," Frank said. "So nothing to worry about."

"Don't ever lie to me again. I don't appreciate walking into a room full of vacationers from another country who could all have had a serious flu virus. You told me they were from Kansas! Fortunately what they had was strep throat and a bad case of sea sickness."

"I don't like your tone."

"And I don't like not knowing what type of situation I'm walking into. I've started them on antibiotics. Keep them away from the other guests for a day or so, and everything should be fine. If something changes, take them to the clinic in Craig to be assessed."

"All right, Cole. Listen. I have a bungalow on the water. It's unoccupied. Why don't you spend the

night here on me? It's eight o'clock and dark out-
side. Dinner's over, but Bubba's still in the kitchen.
I'll have him bring you something to eat at the bar.
Everything will be on the house."

"I'll be sending a bill for the services rendered,"
Cole reminded him.

"And I'll pay it."

"All right. I am rather tired and hungry."

"So you'll keep this outbreak of strep between
you and me?" Frank seemed worried.

"I have to. No laws were broken. The guests
have the right to get sick. I want you to know I
checked their visas, Frank. They have to be out of
the country by Sunday. Make sure they are." Cole
looked at him coldly. "If you need me, I'll be in
the bar."

"I'll have one of the girls bring you the key to
your bungalow."

Cole left Frank and followed the beautifully lit
path surrounded by ancient pines and ferns to the
bar. He took a deep breath of the invigorating air,
the clean smell of wet earth and pine. The night
sky was glorious, brimming with stars.

He was grateful he didn't have to fly back home
on such a magnificent night. He'd pulled an all-
nighter at the hospital the night before and was
beat.

The bar looked like a saloon from the gold-
mining days at the turn of the twentieth century. He
walked inside and could see people sitting at tables

and the bar laughing and talking, while a handful of others danced to the music blaring from a jukebox.

SASHI HANSEN WAS EXHAUSTED as she headed to the bar. Her job was to give a key to a VIP at the resort. Who *wasn't* an important guest here? Then she smiled. Everyone considered themselves important, she supposed.

She lifted a hand to her nose. It smelled of soap. She often worried she'd grown so used to the smell of fish on her skin that she couldn't smell it anymore. Sashi had been in Alaska only a week when she'd overheard how much money could be made working down in the cannery. It paid three times what other jobs paid, but you really had to work hard. Fourteen-hour days on your feet cleaning, filleting and packing fish ready to be sent to places all over the world. So she resigned from her original job as a hotel maid and went to work in the packing plant.

Today Sashi had packed fish all day and the smell had been dreadful. When wasn't it dreadful? She was convinced she was slowly turning into a fish, not realizing how vain she was. The boss had ordered her to wait tables for two more hours. She needed to concentrate on that and then she could hit her bunk bed.

As long as Sashi kept her vision in mind, the long days weren't that bad. She could scarcely believe she was so close to attaining her dream. After working incredibly hard this summer, she'd earned enough money for a down payment on her own dance studio back home in Alexandria, Virginia, and would now be eligible to apply for a business loan. Soon she would be able to open it.

The long hours were draining, but she'd spent worse days getting ready for performances at the Joffrey Ballet School in New York. Not to mention there were only three more days left at this place and then she and her best friend, Kendra, would be flying home. She couldn't wait!

Sashi walked into the bar, ducked behind the counter and found an apron to tie around her waist. Reaching into her jeans, she grabbed a rubber band and pulled her strawberry-blond hair into a ponytail. It reached halfway down her back.

With that accomplished, she inhaled deeply. *Just think about tips.*

First she needed to find a Dr. Stevens. Mac, the bartender, would know him. The middle-aged Tlingit knew everyone who flew in and out of here for whatever reason. "Yo, Mac," she called. "I need some help over here." Over the past three months she'd picked up the easy local banter.

"How can I help you, New York?" he responded.

Sashi had grown accustomed to every employee calling her "New York." After living in the Big Apple for the past ten years, she'd picked up the accent, and here it had earned her the nickname.

"I need to find a Dr. Stevens," she said.

"Really? Did you get lined up for a date?" Mac's brown eyes twinkled.

She blushed. "No. Mr. Marshall told me to give him the key to his bungalow."

"Not anything else?"

Sashi hated all the attention men gave her, even in a teasing manner. "You're shameless." She put her hands on her hips and tried her best to make a hundred pounds look tough.

"I know. But you still love me." Then he gave her a hug. Sashi found if she held herself stiffly, most men let her go pretty fast. And he did.

"Just show me where the doctor is."

Mac brought his face close to hers. He reeked of alcohol, causing her to shudder. "He's the blond guy in the sweater and jeans staring at you." He pointed.

Sashi turned and met the most unusual pair of eyes she'd ever seen—golden like honey, in a face that looked like it belonged in a magazine. Tanned, with an aquiline nose and chiseled features, even a cleft chin. *Damn.* For the first time since she'd been here, she felt her stomach tighten up over a good-looking man. Embarrassed because of the way she was reacting to him, she looked down at the floor.

"New York," Mac said. "Doc Stevens is right there!" He gave her a little shove.

Sashi was sure she was bright red by now. The curse of pale skin.

Stop it, Sashi. Go give the doctor his key!

His table wasn't far from the bar. She pulled

herself together and crossed to him. In an effort to appear in control, she focused on a spot behind his broad shoulders and not on his handsome face. Her heart was pounding too hard. This kind of thing didn't happen to her.

"Welcome to the Watering Hole, Dr. Stevens." Now she met his gaze. Whew! His eyes were a luminous gold. She reached into her pocket and pulled out the key. "I believe this is for you." As she handed it to him she said, "Mr. Marshall wanted me to tell you 'thanks again.'"

As the doctor took the key, his hand brushed hers. She felt a jolt of energy from her fingertips to her midsection.

Sashi had heard of love at first sight, or what she preferred to call *lust* at first sight, but had never believed in it. She chalked it up to living in New York. Or maybe never having a relationship last. Whatever the reason, it had turned her into a real cynic about romance—until this moment. She'd never felt such attraction. No doubt it was one-sided, but it was shocking nevertheless.

"Thank you, Sashi," he replied.

"Oh! You're welcome." She smiled. "It's part of the job. Hey—how do you know my name?"

Suddenly the two most adorable creases bracketed his mouth. "It's on your name tag."

"Of course." She felt herself blush again and bit her lip, continuing to look at him as he looked right back at her. Needing to break the silence, she asked, "Can I get you anything to drink?"

"I'll have whatever you think is the best on tap."

"Are you a lager kind of guy?"

"Always."

"Then I'll be right back." Sashi started to make an escape and compose her thoughts.

"Wait."

Her body quickened. This weird attraction was well beyond her comfort zone. She needed to talk to Kendra right now! Unfortunately, Kendra was with Freddy Marshall, a shameless ladies' man. Sashi detested him, but his father was the boss, so she kept her feelings quiet. What baffled her was how Kendra could be in love with a man who kept breaking her heart.

Sashi had no choice but to turn back to the doctor. "Is there something else I can get you, Dr. Stevens?"

The man leaned back in the chair, his long legs stretched out before him. Was there anything unappealing about him? "First off, call me Cole. Everyone does. Up here we're a pretty informal bunch." He smiled warmly.

Sashi's throat went dry. Maybe this wasn't just a one-way attraction. "Okay—Cole."

He looked at her curiously. "Where are you from? East Coast?"

"Originally from Virginia, but I've spent the past ten years in New York."

He sat up to lean closer to her. "That's why your accent sounds so familiar. A colleague of mine is from New York. He sounds like you."

"Everyone calls me 'New York' up here."

"What did you do there, if I may ask?"

Sashi wondered if the wheat-colored hair that fell over his forehead was soft to the touch. "Pardon?"

"I asked what you did in New York."

"Oh. I studied ballet. Um…let me go and get you that drink."

Sashi headed back to the bar to get his beer, chastising herself for acting like a teenager around him. Get your act together, girl. *He's a customer who wants a beer. That's all.* With that little pep talk, she headed back to his table with the beer.

"Oh, dear," she muttered to herself. This wasn't going to be easy. The man was too damned sexy.

Sashi put his drink on the wooden table. "One lager on the house, courtesy of Mr. Marshall. Is there anything else you would like, Doc—I mean Cole?"

He took a swig of his drink, then set it down. "This is good." He flashed her another warm smile.

"So I've been told." Sashi felt herself smile back.

"You're not a beer drinker, then?"

Sashi wrinkled her nose. "I've never been a fan of beer. Too many calories."

He studied her. "Like you need to worry. So what do you drink?"

Her heart raced from all his attention. "If I do...a gin and tonic."

"Cole!" Mac yelled from the bar. "Stop hitting on the staff!"

"Then stop hiring such good-looking women!" Cole fired back.

Sashi could feel her cheeks burning again. She had to get away. She flashed Cole a smile, then moved to other customers and began taking orders. She couldn't risk jeopardizing her job, not with only three days left. For the past three months she'd spurned every man who'd come on to her, be it an employee or guest.

She needed to ignore this attraction. But it did make her feel better to know she wasn't completely frozen inside, as the men she'd turned down had told her. She guessed she simply wasn't attracted to most men. Only to one blond god with tawny eyes.

The rest of the shift passed quickly. When the doctor ordered another lager or asked her a question, Sashi did her best to look unaffected.

SINCE THAT RED-HAIRED beauty had appeared, Cole sat at the table thunderstruck by what had transpired. Women like that didn't just walk into saloons up in Alaska every day. Was she one of the girls Freddy had brought up from Washington, D.C., under the pretense of proposing to her?

Even if she *was* interested in Freddy, there'd been a spark between Cole and her when their eyes had met. Cole needed to catch her alone before he left the bar in order to find out if this attraction was only in his mind.

He waited outside for the place to close down and for Sashi to come out. Such an unusual name. He wondered what it meant. Hell, he had a ton of questions. Most of all he needed to see her again. She looked like a medieval princess with her porcelain skin and shiny, long hair. And her face! It was beautiful.

He heard the door open before he saw silhouettes moving in the semidarkness. Sashi was the first out. Mac followed after locking up the bar.

"Get a good night's sleep, New York."

"You, too, Mac."

Sashi headed in a different direction than Mac. Cole hoped she wouldn't think he was a stalker. If she screamed and told him to get lost, he would. But if she had felt the same spark he had earlier, she might be happy to see him. No matter. He would keep his distance so she wouldn't feel scared.

"New York!" Cole called out softly when she was near enough. "You never told me where you studied ballet."

SASHI'S HEAD WHIPPED AROUND. There he was, standing on the other side of the bridge she needed to cross to reach her bunkhouse. Was he waiting for her? Her heart leaped at the thought. She hoped he was.

If it had been any other man, she would have been alarmed and called security—all she had to do was reach down to the two-way radio attached to the hem of her jeans and call them. Instead, she was thrilled Cole had wanted to stay and talk to her.

So she leaned against the other side of the arched bridge that ran over one of the various streams on the property. The lights below the bridge cast a romantic aura over the lush forest, making onlookers feel they'd entered the land of Fey. The sky was filled with stars.

"I studied at the Joffrey Ballet School."

There was enough light for Sashi to see Cole's tall frame. He must be at least six-two or -three, with the body of an athlete. She started to imagine what it would be like to be held in arms like those.

"I don't know much about dance," he said. "Could you tell me more about the school?"

She sighed, then said, "It's one of the most prestigious ballet schools in the country."

"You look like a dancer," he said.

"And you're an expert on the subject?" Sashi couldn't keep the sarcasm out of her voice.

Cole took a step closer. "To be honest, speaking from a doctor's point of view, you look like you've been working out for years. Even serving drinks in jeans and a windbreaker, you hold yourself with poise and grace."

Sashi chuckled. "How many dancers do you know? I think you're just teasing me."

A big smile appeared. "So what's a prima ballerina doing out here at a fisherman's paradise?" His voice was deep.

Sashi took a few steps onto the bridge so she could lean over and look into the water rushing below. "I'm sure you've heard the phrase 'Those who can, *do,* and those who can't, *teach.*'" She turned to face him.

"I have," he replied.

"I'm going to let you in on a little secret." She lowered her voice. "I want to open my own dance studio. I love working with children."

Sashi wondered how many women this doctor had known in his life. He was a natural flirt. Suddenly she decided it didn't matter. It wouldn't hurt her to flirt back for once in her life, especially when she knew it could go nowhere.

Cole raked a hand through his thick hair. "I'm still trying to understand how you're going to teach ballet up here."

Sashi stood up straight. "I'm not going to teach here. I plan on opening a studio in Virginia. But I need money to get it started."

"Ah. So you came here to Alaska to earn the big bucks."

"We call it the gold mine down in the plant. Yet the experience of traveling to the last frontier has been life-changing." She smiled at him.

"You work in the packaging plant?" Cole's voice had an edge to it.

She chuckled. "You have a problem with that?"

Cole rubbed his chin. "No… I have great respect for you. Damn. I worked in a cannery one summer and it was tough work."

"Tough work that pays very well," Sashi countered. "Now it's my turn."

"For what?"

"To ask questions." Sashi walked closer to him. "How does an Alaskan bush doctor know the term 'prima ballerina'? Have you even been to a ballet?"

"That's a little harsh. Not all Alaskans are rednecks. And yes, I've gone to ballets." Cole stood up straight.

"Really. Which one is your favorite?"

Cole reached her in two quick strides. The heat of his body mixed with the tangy spice of his cologne began to break down her walls. He lifted his hand to tilt her face up to him. "My favorite is *The Sleeping Beauty*."

Sashi stared into his face and gulped. Those eyes were intoxicating. Their color seemed to change constantly. Out here on the bridge it was like honey. At this point she knew she was in way over her head, but at the moment she didn't care. His lips were full and his jaw had a five o'clock shadow she longed to touch.

Was this love at first sight? Or just pure lust? She knew she was beyond any coherent thought at the moment. Having had such little experience with men, she wished she knew what was going on. She had to go on instinct alone.

THIS INTENSE ATTRACTION caught Cole off guard. He'd heard his friends talk of love at first sight and he'd never believed them. But as he reached out and pulled her into his arms, it seemed the most natural thing in the world to do. "Have you ever danced in that particular ballet?"

"Yes," she answered in a whisper, "but never as the prima ballerina."

Cole bent his head down until their mouths met. At first their kisses were soft and gentle, and Sashi touched her fingers to his jaw. As passion filled his veins, Cole deepened the kiss and pulled her closer, releasing her magnificent hair.

Sashi's body trembled as Cole kissed her with a new intensity. Every touch was more erotic as his lips and tongue slanted deeply, seeking a closeness only full sexual union could satisfy. He wanted to take her to his bungalow now and make love to her.

Show some control, Cole, he told himself. *You can't just ravage the woman.* He wrapped his arms around her waist and rested his head on hers. He was sure she could hear his heart pounding.

"Sashi," he said, panting, "I'm a man who is usually in control of himself. But I'm losing the battle. What would you like to do? I'll respect your decision."

He looked into her glowing emerald eyes, awaiting her reply.

Chapter Two

"I...I don't know," she said. "I've never felt this way before."

Sashi trembled from pure excitement. She tightened her arms around Cole's neck and kissed him deeply. He seemed to lose the control he'd been trying so hard to keep. He groaned and pinned her body against the bridge railing, returning her kiss.

Over the years Sashi had heard her friends talk about moments like this. She hadn't believed they'd actually let a man they didn't know near them. But now she understood. Tonight out here, she couldn't imagine not letting him touch her. She never wanted to let him go.

They stayed on the bridge, kissing and caressing, unable to get enough of each other, for the next thirty minutes, until at last Sashi gently pushed him away, saying she had a long day tomorrow. As promised, he accepted her decision.

After leaving him, Sashi could hear music blaring from her bunkhouse before she walked into the bare, A-frame cabin. Kendra must have alerted the four other girls she was absent. They shared the same bunk room.

Damn.

They must all be waiting for her. She touched her fingers to her lips. They felt swollen from all the kissing. Her time with Cole had been so intense, she'd lost track of time.

Reaching for the doorknob, she took a deep breath and walked into the room to face the women she'd come to know over the summer.

"Sashi? Where have you been?" Kendra threw a pillow at her. "Do you know how worried I was?"

Sashi easily evaded the pillow, diverting it to Natalie's bed. "I'm sorry. I lost track of time."

Sarah, a busty young blonde who, like all the others, was after Freddy, chimed in. "Somebody looks like they've been making out!"

The cabin erupted in shrieks, causing Sashi to turn red.

"I've got to see this," Bridgette declared. She got off her bed and moved in on Sashi for a closer inspection.

Bridgette was tall and curvy with long blond hair. Freddy liked all types of women. He'd hurt Kendra when he'd brought her up here letting her think she was the only woman he cared for. Little did Kendra realize she'd be competing with four others!

"Can you guys just leave me alone?" Sashi said.

"No!" Bridgette declared. "You've been Little Miss Goody Two-Shoes all summer and this is pretty exciting."

"Go back to sleep." Sashi rolled her eyes and headed over to her bed.

"Hold on just a second!" Blake called out.

Sashi groaned. No. Not Blake Carrey, the beast from Boston with the looks of a movie star and blond hair cut to her chin. Kendra knew that Blake's perfectly tanned body came out of a spray bottle from France and her personality came straight from hell. Blake had made Kendra's life miserable up here. She was obsessed with Freddy and convinced he was going to propose to her this summer.

"What do you want, Blake?"

"Who's the guy? What makes him so special? Come on. Tell us."

Sashi turned around to face the woman. She didn't care much for Blake, whose constant complaining over the hard work got on everyone's nerves.

With a smile she said, "He's none of your business."

"Don't tell me you finally got it on with Mac!" Blake stood in front of her in satin pajamas that seemed so out of place up here in Alaska.

Sashi laughed. "Oh, if you only knew the truth." At that she turned around and began to get things out of her bag. "Why don't you go back to bed, Blakey? You need your beauty sleep."

Sashi left for the latrine/shower house with her bag of toiletries. She needed to brush her teeth and wash her face. It was amazing how the guests got indoor plumbing and every modern amenity, while the workers lived back in time. Mr. Marshall had never gotten around to bringing the workers' cabins into the twentieth century, never mind the twenty-first.

As she walked the short distance to the latrine, she heard laughter. But a loud bang from the door made her turn around to see who'd followed her. "Kendra! You scared me!"

Her tall friend caught up with her in seconds. "Sashi, what the hell? You've never done this before. You've got to tell me what happened earlier."

"I'm sorry. But I met the hottest man ever."

Kendra stopped walking and stared at Sashi in the moonlight. "Are you drunk? Is this the same Sashi I grew up with?"

Sashi didn't want to stand out in the dark. This was bear country and she knew the rules, so she continued to walk. "Seriously, Kendra, you have to swear not to tell the girls."

They reached the smelly outbuilding that serviced the employees' needs. She headed in and Kendra followed. "Sashi, you and I don't like any of those girls except Natalie. Who would I tell?"

"You'd tell Freddy!"

"Not true. I can keep secrets."

"Promise?" Sashi's heart was pounding as she washed her hands.

Kendra sounded exasperated. "Pinkie-promise."

"Okay." Sashi started to change clothes. "There was this hot bush doctor who flew up from Ketchikan today. His name is—"

"Dr. Stevens." Kendra finished the sentence for her.

She felt a wave of jealously sweep through her. When had Kendra met him? Sashi was only half-dressed in her thermal top. "How do you know him?"

Kendra laughed. "Girl, you look so upset! I was working at the reception desk when he arrived and I took him to Mr. Marshall. He was pretty hot."

Sashi nodded. "Yeah."

"I'm not going to tell you anything more until *you* tell me how far you went."

"We only kissed. I didn't want to do more. He's asked to see me again." Sashi disappeared back into one of the toilet cubicles.

"How are you guys going to meet again?" Kendra asked.

"He's a bush doctor, and he'll fly out here and take us to Ketchikan early on the day we're supposed to fly home. Then he's going to take us to lunch. He says he can get us to the airport fast, too."

"Do you believe him?"

"Of course."

"Well, you're going to have to call him and change the plans."

"Why?"

"Because I broke off with Freddy and have booked us a three-day tour of Prince of Wales Island."

Sashi emerged from the cubicle ready for bed. "Kendra, I can't afford a trip like that."

"I know. That's why it's my treat. The tour's all about the Native Americans who lived here on this island. Our guide is an Native chief who knows amazing sites. It's going to be incredible."

Sashi went over and hugged her friend. She felt for her. Kendra had been fighting for Freddy's attention all summer and finally learned from co-workers in the packing plant that he was just a player who brought his women up here to work. Worse, he put all of them in the same cabin!

"I'm proud of you for the way you're handling this, Kendra," Sashi said. "I'll call Cole in the morning and find out if I can see him some other way before we leave Alaska."

"I've never seen you this keen on a guy before," Kendra said in a soft tone.

"I know it's crazy. Cole was talking about flying out to Virginia for a vacation to see me. I didn't know what to say other than I'd love it."

"Stranger things have happened. I'm happy for you, Sashi. Now I've just got to get over Freddy."

"I'll help you."

THE RAIN WAS COMING DOWN in sheets as Cole drove his Range Rover. If he hadn't been on this road over a hundred times before, he didn't think he'd find his house high on the hill overlooking Ketchikan.

At last he pulled into his driveway. With a push of a button, the garage door swung open and he drove inside. The door immediately closed behind him, locking out the storm. He hoped the weatherman had been right and it would clear up fast. He was looking forward to flying out and seeing Sashi and her friend the day after tomorrow.

Cole rested his head against the steering wheel for a second. He'd never fallen for a woman this fast. His body could still feel her in his arms. What was he getting himself into?

Just then his phone buzzed. He didn't recognize the number. Maybe it was Sashi. His heart raced at the thought of talking to her. "Dr. Stevens," he said.

"Cole. It's Sashi."

Her voice sounded as sexy on the phone as it did in real life. "Hey there, New York. How are you doing?"

"I'm fine. It's…good to hear your voice."

"So what's going on?"

"Well, there's been a little change in plans."

Cole felt his stomach knot. "Like what?"

"Nothing bad. Remember how I told you I came up here with my best friend?"

"Uh-huh."

"She totally surprised me by offering me a free

tour of the island with her. It'll extend my stay for another three days."

"Wait—your friend bought you a tour?" Cole was incredulous.

"Okay. I'm not putting you on. Kendra has lots of money, and this trip has been horrible for her. Freddy Marshall lied about his intentions when he brought her up here."

"Oh, I know all about Freddy Marshall and his lies, but I'm still trying to figure out why you're evading me."

"No! That's not it at all. Kendra has her degree in anthropological studies from George Washington University. She's trying to salvage this trip by turning the last days into something good. That's why she paid for me to come along with her on this three-day getaway. She wants to forget Freddy and focus on something positive."

"What does this trip entail?" Cole was trying to keep his voice calm.

"We're going to be making a small survey of where the Tlingit and Haida Natives lived on Prince of Wales Island. We'll head south to Hydaburg to see the totem poles and study some ancient sites in the area. Then we'll head north to the cave El Capitan, where we'll go spelunking to find ancient petroglyphs."

"That sounds amazing." Cole tried to keep the disappointment out of his voice. He was thirty-five, for Pete's sake, not some schoolboy. "Will you need a flight in from the island, or will the tour end in Ketchikan?"

"The tour ends in Ketchikan. I told the guide I wanted to get in early so we would have a six-hour layover. Do you think you'll have time to see me and my friend then?"

Cole found his first smile of the day. The E.R. had been a mess because of the storm, and he'd been wondering what would happen with Sashi. Now he knew he'd be able to see her again. "All you have to do is let me know what airport you land at and I'll be waiting for you."

"Okay, that sounds great."

"Look, you're too special to let go. Have fun, New York. I'll see you in a couple of days. Promise me you'll be safe. It's bear country out there."

"I know. I've been living in it for three months."

"Take care, anyway."

"Bye," Sashi said softly.

"Miss you already, New York." Then Cole clicked off.

It was a beautiful morning to be leaving Marshall's. The sun had turned the water along the coastline turquoise-blue. Sashi could hear sea lions barking in the distance. The majesty of Alaska was something she would never forget, and the huge paycheck she'd just wired home to her bank really made her stay up here worth it. She felt giddy knowing she'd earned enough to get a business loan to open up her dance studio. She finally had a place in the world where she belonged.

She got busy loading up Kendra's and her gear into their guide's plane. He was Joe Running Bear, an older Native chief with black hair peppered with white, whom she found very kind and apparently happy to do this tour.

Kendra was still having a hard time saying goodbye to Freddy even though she claimed she'd broken up with him. Why she continued to spend time with that weasel was beyond Sashi's comprehension.

Sure he was good-looking, if you liked pretty boy features, calculating blue eyes and a tall wiry frame. But when you got past his looks, he had nothing else. He was a phony, just stringing every girl on. Now Kendra was standing next to him, part of his usual fawning entourage of women and men.

Finally Kendra emerged from the mob. She seemed happy. Obviously something had just happened between Freddy and her friend.

"Why are you all smiles?" Sashi asked directly.

Kendra didn't look at her. "Joe? Are we ready to go?"

"Yes, we are."

"Great! Come on, Sashi," Kendra called out as she climbed into the pontoon plane secured to the dock. "I'll tell you inside."

Sashi had a bad feeling. What had Freddy promised Kendra now? What had she gotten herself into?

The door closed and Joe climbed into the pilot's seat. He told them to put on their seat belts along with headphones so they could talk. He started the engine and soon they were taxiing over the water, then lifting in the air. Both girls stared out the windows, caught up in the splendor of Prince of Wales Island. Sashi found this land, covered in a rain forest of ferns and pines, magical. Bears and bald eagles made their home there, and whales dotted the coastline.

Before they touched down at their first site, Kendra grabbed Sashi's hand. "We have to talk."

Sashi didn't want to stop looking out the window. "So *now* you feel like talking?"

"I'm going to have Joe fly us up to a lake called Red Bay. Freddy, Bridgette, Natalie, Nick and George are going to fly out for a goodbye party at the cabin located right on the lake. It's all been arranged."

Sashi bit her lip. She didn't really care for Nick or George. They were two local guys from Craig who worked the fishing boats and had big crushes on the two other girls. "Why? I thought you called it off with Freddy."

"I did, but today he begged me for a second chance. I couldn't say no." Kendra's eyes began to well up with tears.

Sashi could see her friend was still madly in love with him. "Okay, we'll do it. I'm just glad Blake isn't coming."

"Me, too. I think Freddy is finally choosing me over Blake. She's been my biggest competition all summer." Kendra reached over and gave Sashi a hug.

Sashi hugged her back. "It's all going to work out fine," she said, but doubted it.

COLE SUTURED A NASTY CUT on his patient's forehead. "Cid, my friend, you really need to listen. Take it easy and lay off the booze. They have to bring you in here way too often."

"I feel your love for me right here in my heart, Doc." The tough fisherman pounded his chest with his fist. The blue eyes of the bar-brawler met the no-nonsense of Cole's rich amber eyes.

"Yeah, Cid. I'm thinking you must have a thing for me by now. Asking for me by name? It's touching." Cole shook his head. "Come on, let's get more personal. I'll even get you a bed here on the rehab floor."

At that comment Cid's fisherman buddies, who'd brought him in, started laughing. "Doc, Cid's a good fisherman *if* he could ever stay out of a bar. More importantly, out of a bet!" His captain, Lee Jarvis, always vouched for him.

Cole turned back to his patient. "Cid's got a drinking problem. I'm worried that one night he might walk off one of your crabbing boats in a drunken stupor straight into the ocean."

"We all have a drinkin' problem. Just sew him

up," Lee said, getting testy. "He's too good of an engineer to lose for the season. I'll look into his problem after we catch our quota."

Cole turned around in his chair. "Is that a promise?"

"No. It's a maybe."

Cole got up and began to strip off his sterile gloves. "Cid, I truly hope to see you in the spring. It would make my Easter dreams come true."

Lee jumped in. "We'll do our best, Doc."

With that Cole left the room and began the long walk from the patients' rooms to the hub of the E.R. He stripped his long body of the rest of the protective clothing and turned his smile on one of the new nurses.

"Stacey? The patient in room three needs another round of meds. Take either Heather or Mildred in with you. The boys can be a rough crew."

Stacey just stared at him.

Cole turned to Mildred, who said, "Come on, Stacey. Let's get you used to the crabbers." But she looked back at Cole and shook her head.

"What?" he said.

"You and that amazing smile of yours. If I were twenty years younger, you'd be mine, Cole."

"I *am* yours, Mildred," he said.

"Don't flirt with me, big boy, even if it still works."

Cole walked away, chuckling to himself. He was looking forward to tomorrow's reunion with Sashi.

"WE'VE ARRIVED, LADIES," Joe Running Bear exclaimed from the cockpit. Speaking into the enormous headphone, he began discussing landing procedures. The plane circled the lake one time, then made its descent toward the pristine waters of Red Bay. The landing was as smooth and soft as silk.

As the plane taxied the two women stared out the cabin windows. A bald eagle who'd stood proud on a tree took off, its magnificent wings spread in flight. Sashi spotted startled Sitka deer moving back from the shore, robins flying to and from their nests, squirrels scampering into the undergrowth. Ancient trees stood in various states of decay. Cedars and spruce covered in moss and lichen peeked out of the morning mist hovering just above the ground.

The sun poked through the clouds, casting a blanket of diamonds over the water. The diamonds shimmered as the plane drew closer to the dock of the Pan-Abode cabin, one of many prefab cabins dotting the Alaskan bush.

Sashi lifted her eyebrows, trying to decide if she dared ask their pilot-cum-tour guide the question on her mind: Had the trees been planted on purpose to look like a wreath around the lake, or had nature created its own perfection? But where questions about Alaska were concerned, she'd learned to keep her mouth shut in case she sounded too naive.

Over the past three months Sashi had learned

Alaska was a land of mystery. It was hard to believe that it was just last March her best friend from childhood had begged her to come up here.

It had all sprung from Kendra's falling in love with Freddy, which had happened when both she and Frank Marshall's son had attended school together in Washington, D.C. Freddy had asked Kendra to come up to the resort and spend time with him. She went because she believed she had found the man she was going to marry, and this time with him would make for a perfect summer.

Kendra had asked Sashi to come because she knew her friend needed the money to make her dream become a reality.

Sashi took in Kendra's silhouette up front. They'd been best friends since they were three years old. Sashi couldn't believe the past twenty-five years had gone by so quickly. During that time Kendra had become a tall, striking woman, one just as beautiful on the inside as she was on the outside. She was one of those rare types of people who would hold some fund-raiser or another for a cause no one had ever heard of just because she cared. Sashi never knew Kendra to be unkind to another soul.

If people thought Kendra was odd, it was only because she was so smart. Kendra had a different way of thinking from most people. Sometimes it made her seem snobby, but nothing could be further from the truth.

"My friends," Joe said through the headphones in his deep, rich voice. "It appears Mother Nature has looked kindly on us this morning. We had the bald eagle to welcome us and the sun to shine on us. We will be docking momentarily. Since no one has arrived yet, we will prepare for a wet docking and hike to the cabin."

"Uh, Joe?" said Kendra. "Can you elaborate on what a wet docking is?"

His eyes twinkled as he looked back. "The parks department hasn't kept up the dock here at the lake. So we have to wade to shore."

Kendra poked Joe in a friendly manner. "Please tell us you have waders."

He laughed. "Nothing to worry about, ladies. Joe takes care of everything."

Kendra and Sashi looked at each other and smiled. On their tour yesterday, Joe had been quite a character, providing them with anecdotes about his ancestors. Then he'd made fun of Kendra's pronunciations of some Tlingit words and told story after story until their stomachs hurt from laughing so hard.

Sashi loved this man's company and thought it was a shame they were cutting their tour short, all because of Freddy. But it wasn't her place to say anything. After all, Kendra was the one paying for this three-day adventure trip with Joe.

For some reason, Sashi feared that this last hurrah in Red Bay would be a disaster. She'd told Ken-

dra that if Freddy Marshall had been serious about
her, he would have wanted to be alone with Kendra. But her friend had refused to listen. She had
insisted she needed to see Freddy and the group
one more time before they left Alaska.

All these thoughts filled Sashi's mind as she
watched Joe exit the plane first and walk up the
slope to the split-level cabin. Once he felt the area
was safe, he called to them. They put on the fishing waders Joe had given them, then grabbed their
night packs.

Kendra got out of the plane ahead of Sashi, visibly bursting with excitement and the knowledge
that Sashi, whose waders were two sizes too big
for her and whose pack weighed half as much as
she did, was going to need help. Sashi watched
her friend walk up the moss- and rock-laden hill.

After throwing down her pack, Kendra returned
to the shore and stood half in, half out of the water.
She grinned as Sashi was planning her next move.

"Sashi, what are you doin'?"

"I'm sitting here thinking of all the predicaments
I've been in this summer. I have to tell you *this* is
a classic." Still clinging to the edge of the plane's
opening, Sashi could tell Kendra was trying hard
not to laugh. Kendra knew Sashi hated depending
on people in any way.

"Would you mind if I go get my camera?" Kendra asked. "We're lucky that it's such a nice day
for the end of August."

"I thought you'd never ask," Sashi said drily. "Go ahead, then maybe you can help me get off this plane."

In a minute Kendra was back with a camera, took a few shots, then helped Sashi wade to shore. They were both laughing as the waders kept smacking Sashi in the face.

Finally the two of them made it into the cabin. Joe had made a fire and had coffee brewing for the three of them. While Kendra kept a vigil at the window waiting for Freddy's plane to appear, Joe took Sashi to the back of the cabin.

She eyed her wily comrade. "What's all this?" He'd been up to something. The old chief possessed the wisdom and the walk of a great tribal leader from the past.

Joe's voice grew hushed as he placed his hands on her shoulders. "*You* remind me of a lone wolf pup. It's in your eyes and in your wild red hair. Just learning about its power and strength is what makes you so strong."

He picked up a small, rectangular handheld device. "My daughter and her husband gave this to me for my birthday. It's a personal locater beacon if there's an emergency. Don't leave the cabin without it."

"But, Joe, don't *you* need it?"

He pulled another one out of his vest.

"Are they connected?" Sashi asked.

He shook his head and his eyes danced with

laughter. "To satellites, yes. Me, no. I have a good friend who is a doctor named Cole Stevens. Like you he is a wolf, also a loner. He never leaves home without one. He got it for me. Same birthday, I think."

"I've met Dr. Stevens. I'm supposed to meet up with him again tomorrow."

Joe's face broke out in a radiant smile. "Ah. He has finally found his mate."

Sashi's face reddened. "Oh, that's a little bit out there, Joe. We just met."

"No, Joe is usually right."

"You've got to be making this up." She loved the way he referred to himself in the third person. She tried not to laugh while she held a hot cup of coffee in her hand.

"I laugh about Joe all the time," he said. "But I never laugh about safety. Never." He held the device in his hand and showed her how to turn it on. With care he explained how each device was coded by its own transmitter signal.

"Here's the funny part," Joe said. "Cole and my daughter are very good friends, but they don't know Joe has *two* devices." By his smile, she knew he enjoyed telling the story. "Since they know I have little faith in modern technology always working, they offer to pay the yearly fee."

Sashi bit her lip, trying to understand this man. "But if you don't trust the devices, then why carry them?"

"Now Joe never said he didn't *trust* the devices." His finger shook, but his smile was back. "I like an extra one in this land of the Raven. Because of this old body, it gives me peace of mind in the back country."

"Where will you be tonight? I don't want to take your peace of mind."

Joe shook his head. "You *want* to take a piece of my mind and keep the device on you." He tucked it into a pocket on her padded vest. "Now let me give you another piece of my mind." For the next ten minutes he told Sashi about bear mace and how to survive in bear country.

"Thank you," she said, then hugged him. "Where are you flying now?"

His eyes lit up. "I'm going back to Ketchikan to be with my daughter, granddaughter and son-in-law."

"Until tomorrow, then."

"I will be here early."

Sashi followed him out of the cabin and down the steep slope. "Can you give me an idea of what time exactly?"

"Depends on the weather." Joe looked up at the sky, then back to her. "As you know, Mother Earth is going into her rainy season. I'll be here about nine." He smiled, waved goodbye and made his way down to the plane. "You worry about me too much, little wolf. I'm the one who's worried about you out here without a gun. I wish you ladies would take one."

"Joe, Freddy's coming and I know he always carries at least two guns. Even so, we know bear safety. Everything will be all right."

With his long, salt-and-pepper hair and beautiful jewelry that shook as he moved, Joe cut an elegant figure out here in nature. He eyed her. "You talk so tough I almost believe you. Then you turn sideways and I forget you even exist."

She put her hands on her hips and laughed.

He gave her one last wave, then began to wade to the plane.

Deep down Sashi wondered if Freddy was really going to come or if he was going to let Kendra down like he'd done so many times. Her heart ached for her friend, but when she remembered tomorrow when she'd see Cole again, the emptiness that had filled her life for so long seemed to fade.

COLE LOOKED AT THE LITTLE GIRL seated on the edge of the hospital bed holding her mom's hand tightly. Her blond hair and big blue eyes reminded him of Jake's daughter. His friend was a lucky man. Cole wasn't a pediatrician, but he'd learned a few tricks to get kids to cooperate.

"So I hear your name is Maggie the Magician." His expression was kind as he looked at this cutie.

The girl shook her head, but then she smiled.

"Let's try again. Is your name Maggie the Magnet?"

"No! You're silly. I'm Maggie Johnson." Her tiny voice had come out in a whisper.

"Wow. I wish my name was Maggie Johnson. Then I'd be really cool like you."

"But you can't because you're an old man." Her voice was firmer now.

Her parents started offering apologies, but Cole just laughed. "I like you, Maggie Johnson. Do you want to come and work here?"

"No. I don't want to leave my mommy."

"Oh. You have a good mommy?"

"I have the best mommy in the world." Her eyes got really big. "And my dad is the best, too." Her face was very serious.

"Well, Maggie, can you tell me how you got hurt?"

"I was throwing horseshoes with my brother."

"Can you show me where your leg hurts?"

Her eyes began to well with tears. "I don't like looking at it."

Cole glanced around the room. "Do you like books?"

"Yes." She lit up.

Cole rolled his chair over to a magazine rack, and stuffed in the back for occasions like this was a kid's book. He pulled it out. "I happen to have a Dora the Explorer book. Do you like Dora?"

"I *am* Dora."

"Oh, I thought you were Maggie."

"I'm both!" The little girl giggled.

Cole handed the book to her mom. "Okay then, Maggie and Dora the Explorer. Can you show me where you hurt?"

The little girl lifted up her skirt to her knee, revealing a cut that clearly needed stitches.

"Okay. Let me get my pack full of stuff to fix your ouchie."

"Will it hurt?"

"Only a tiny bit, I promise."

As Cole sewed up Maggie's leg, his mind began to dwell on Sashi. Was she okay? What was she doing? He couldn't wait to kiss her again.

Chapter Three

Sashi went into the two-story A-frame cabin to join Kendra. She decided their summer's rigorous work schedule still hadn't been as hard as working for a real dance company. And the fourteen- to sixteen-hour workdays did mean more money, although Kendra had just about died trying to keep up and had lost ten pounds this summer.

As soon as the reality of their situation had taken hold, Kendra probably would have left if she hadn't known Sashi needed the money so desperately. It had been fortunate for Sashi that Kendra had decided to follow Freddy up here. Last spring she'd broached the idea with Sashi of coming up to Alaska for fun, friendship, adventure and money.

Stepping over their gear, Sashi made a mental note to put the gear away after she'd had a talk with Kendra. But she couldn't find her.

"Kendra?" No answer. Her friend must have gone to the outhouse. "Ahh, rustic joys of Alaskan life," Sashi muttered.

As she started out the door to look for her, Kendra suddenly pushed past her with eyes full of tears. She ran to the window seat. "I don't think he's coming."

Sashi sat beside her friend. Tears gushed down Kendra's cheeks. Sashi grabbed the bandanna she'd been carrying in her pocket and began to dab at her friend's face.

"What's going on, Kendra? Tell me."

Kendra looked at her before she closed her eyes and breathed deeply. "I just know Freddy isn't going to come. It's already three o'clock. If he were going to be here, I think he'd have shown up by now."

Sashi looked into her friend's big brown eyes. How could there be so much sadness? "I bet he's just running late. I've never seen a guy who lived as much on the edge as Freddy."

At that moment they heard the sound of a plane coming in.

Kendra jumped up and ran out of the cabin, Sashi following. "It's Freddy!" Kendra cried. "He came." And sure enough, within seconds Freddy's plane made its descent onto the unspoiled lake.

As the group who had come for the night disembarked from the plane, Sashi saw her friend stop in her tracks.

"What's going on?" Sashi asked her. "Why did you stop?"

Kendra gestured in the direction of the plane. Sashi looked and instantly knew. Freddy was unloading the plane, yet he hugged Blake every chance he got.

"Is this a joke?" Sashi was taken aback. She stared at her friend.

Kendra's eyes filled with tears. "Obviously it's not," she said. Kendra turned and walked back into the cabin.

There was something different about Kendra today, Sashi thought, something more than her friend just being hurt by Freddy's actions once again. Sashi couldn't quite put her finger on it, but it was there.

Over the next hour the group unloaded the plane and had the cabin ready for their big going-away party tonight. It was to be a keg party. Keggers were extremely childish affairs to Sashi, even though she'd been to many as a young college student. She wouldn't have thought it was the right kind of party to have out in the middle of the Alaskan bush!

Sure it was fun to see Natalie, Bridgette and the boys. But when she saw Freddy with his hands all over Blake, Sashi was appalled. How could someone be so cruel? Why didn't he just let Kendra go?

The large cabin easily held the group of eight. When most of the crowd started their partying, Sashi went to look for Kendra. She found her crying on a bench overlooking the lake.

"Kendra, all I have to say is Freddy is an SOB! At least you found out now and not later when you got closer to him."

"Sashi, you don't understand all that's going on here." Kendra looked at Sashi helplessly.

"Then explain it to me," Sashi said.

"I can't. I have to talk to Freddy first. But right now I'm too tired."

"All right. Why don't we go take a nap and you can talk to Freddy later. I know you were up at five this morning. And then let's go explore those limestone caves near the cabin Joe told us about. Apparently some of them have petroglyphs few people have ever seen."

The two of them headed into the cabin loft and within minutes Kendra was snuggled into her sleeping bag and fast asleep. Sashi crawled into her own sleeping bag, thinking that looking at caves sounded just like the kind of thing her friend needed to do in order to get her mind off Freddy. And a nap might help clear her thoughts and get her back in tune with herself. Soon Sashi drifted off.

When she woke up, the light was dimming. What time was it? She checked her watch. Seven o'clock.

She stretched and looked over at her friend's bunk. It was empty. Kendra must have got up and gone downstairs. Sashi climbed out of her sleeping bag and quickly threw on a thermal vest. The temperature in the cabin was beginning to drop. Her cross trainers were next to her. She put them on and headed downstairs.

The main room was warm but full of people acting like fools. Sashi walked up to Bridgette. "Do you know where Kendra is?"

With blurry eyes and a silly smile, Bridgette pointed to the back bedroom. "In there." Bridgette began to sway back and forth to the music of the guitar one of the guys had brought.

Sashi headed back to the bedroom, where she could hear loud voices. She tried to open the door but it was locked. "Kendra? Are you okay?"

In a flash, eyes wide, Kendra flew out of the bedroom, through the main room, then right out the door. She took off at a brisk pace and Sashi struggled to keep up with her.

"Kendra, what's going on? What were you and Freddy fighting about? Where are you going?"

"I just need to get out of the house! Apparently Freddy proposed to Blake! I can't take it anymore!"

Now that it was almost September, the days were getting shorter. It would be dark soon, and it was imperative Sashi get them back to the cabin. The later it got, the greater their chances of encountering bears. It was after seven o'clock.

The emerald rain forest had taken on darker hues. Sashi could hear ravens, eagles, larks and other types of wildlife in the bush. The canopy of tall cedars and aspen was dense and she couldn't see the sky.

Kendra had charged on ahead. To reach her, Sashi had to bat her way through a grouping of hemlocks, then climb a grassy slope to a copse of trees, where there was a jutting of rock concealing limestone caves. Finally she caught up to Kendra again. Sashi tapped her on the shoulder to let her know she was there.

Kendra turned to her, but her face suddenly froze in terror.

"What's wrong?"

"B-b-b-ear!" She screamed.

Sashi stood still. She realized they'd broken every rule in the guidebooks and she didn't even have any bear mace on her.

"Kendra, we need to be calm and speak softly," she whispered. "If that doesn't work, we need to fight and yell because black bears don't give up that easily."

"Okay, Sashi," Kendra whispered. "But it's staring at me. It's going to kill my baby!"

"You're *pregnant?* How long have you known?" Sashi asked.

"Two weeks, but tonight Freddy denied it's his."

The next few minutes happened fast. Sashi watched in terror as Kendra took off, running down the other side of the hill into a hemlock forest, where she tried to climb a big alder tree. A sow with cubs would chase her and follow her up.

"No, Kendra! No!"

She had to stop the bear, save her friend. Without a second thought she threw herself in its way. The sow barely noticed her. In the next instant, the eight-foot, salmon-fed animal tossed her in the air, bruising her back and slicing open her left upper arm. Upon landing, Sashi's right foot hit the ground first and twisted as her body fell at an angle.

She could only lift her right arm in a futile attempt to prevent her head from hitting a rock on the ground. Fortunately the rock just grazed her temple. Lying facedown on the dirt, she could barely think. The pain radiating from her lower leg was excruciating.

Sashi knew she had to move and get away from the bear in case it came back. She clawed her way into a nearby cave, dank and cold as a tomb. Too terrified to scream, she curled into a ball on the floor, then craned her neck to see if the bear was there.

No, it wasn't. It had gone. Where was Kendra? Was she safe?

She prayed.

She realized she needed to start taking care of herself or she was going to die. She counted to three in her mind and then turned herself over. The pain was unbearable.

Her leg was much worse than she'd thought, probably broken, but right now her main concern was her left arm, which was bleeding profusely. She had to stop it. Using her teeth and right hand, she ripped off a piece of her shirt, which she then somehow managed to tie using her bad arm. At last she got a piece big enough to tie around the cut to stem the flow. It took a few tries to get the rough bandage tight, but she fought through silent tears and sweat, and it worked. Then she relaxed her body and calmed her breathing, and soon she fell asleep from exhaustion.

She awoke later with a start. "Oh, God, where am I?" Then she remembered and began to shake. She could hear the howl of a wolf in the distance. *Breathe, Sashi. You've danced for years. Pain is part of being a dancer.*

Where was the group? Maybe Cole would come and find her. He was a bush doctor. Her breathing slowed and she slept again.

When she came to this time, her thoughts were reeling. *I'll be strong for Kendra and her baby and my parents. I'm their only child and they need me.* Thirsty, she turned her head and tried to lick the water trickling down the middle of the cave floor. *Yes, I will be found.*

She tried to move her right foot, but couldn't. She cried silent tears. *I don't want to die. I'm not going to die. I will dance again. Please God, save me.*

She called for her friend. "Kendra? Kendra? Kendra?" Her voice grew hoarse. She refused to think no one could hear her in this cave.

IN A DREAM, COLE COULD HEAR his name being said over and over again. A knock on the door alerted him that he was needed in the E.R. He jumped out of the makeshift hospital bed that was on hand for the emergency room doctors. He slipped on his Crocs and grabbed his white jacket.

From years of practice he flipped on the light switch, then headed over to the sink to brush his teeth and splash some water on his face. He sure hoped he had time to go home and properly shower before he saw Sashi today. As soon as she called, he would be off duty. Trading schedules with Dr. Reagan, he'd done the all-night shift. It was worth it. He couldn't wait to see her.

"Paging Dr. Stevens, Dr. Cole Stevens. Please report to the E.R. desk immediately. That's Dr. Stevens, Dr. Cole Stevens." He rushed out the door and headed down the hall, hoping it wasn't a terrible trauma. He didn't want any distractions on his day off. Once at the emergency desk, he picked up the phone. "This is Dr. Stevens."

"Cole, this is Chief Hunter with the Alaska State Troopers on Prince of Wales Island."

"Trace. I know who you are. I'm just trying to figure out why in the hell you're being so formal with me." He leaned against the high wraparound desk.

"We've got ourselves a bad situation. I think you're the twentieth person I've called today."

Cole chuckled and turned toward the wall to keep his voice from carrying. "You waited that long to get a doctor on board for whatever problem you've gotten yourself into?"

"This isn't a laughing matter. Two women have gone missing. Joe Running Bear, Freddy Marshall and his friends are very worried about their situation."

"How is Joe involved in this?" Cole was afraid something might have happened to Joe's daughter or one of her friends. He rubbed his whiskered jaw in frustration.

"It's not like that. He's taken some twenty or so city ladies on one of his Native tours."

Cole frowned. "I didn't know Joe got people to go on those anymore. The guy charges a fortune. Last I heard it was two years ago since someone booked."

"Well, you know Joe," the chief said, warming to the subject. "Once in a while someone will pay and off he goes. Apparently he just adores these women."

"Are they Tlingit?" he questioned.

"No. White girls from Arlington, Virginia."

Cole's stomach fell to the floor. "Do you have names?"

"Why? Do you know the women?"

"Maybe."

"I've got a Kendra Knight and a Sashi Hansen. Sound familiar?"

"Yes." Cole tried to shut off the fear that racked his system.

"I'm sorry. I didn't know you knew anyone up at Marshall's. All I can say is, you need to fly out here as soon as possible. You're our best bush doctor. We've got a lot of caves here. Thank heaven you and Joe have hours of spelunking behind you."

Cole looked at his watch. Noon. "How bad is it?"

"Freddy and some friends met the two women

out there yesterday. This morning when Joe arrived, he woke the six-person party from their sleep. Knight and Hansen weren't there. Their bags had never been opened for a change of clothes. Nobody knows or remembers what happened last night."

"If the weather holds, I'll try to be there in an hour. Do you have spelunking gear on hand?"

"That's a go. Thanks, Cole."

"No problem. See you, Trace."

Cole looked at his watch again—12:05. He could be out to Red Bay by one-thirty at the latest.

HE DECIDED TO DO A GRAND SWEEP of the Red Bay Lake vicinity in his Cessna. It was vital he get an idea of the terrain where the search-and-rescue would be working. He radioed Jake for coordinates and more information. Unfortunately his friend had nothing else to tell him.

His thoughts kept returning to Sashi, that beautiful woman who'd entranced him just a few nights ago. How could he be doing a search-and-rescue for her today? He was supposed to be meeting her for a date! He prayed to God nothing bad had happened to her or her friend.

It brought back painful memories from another time and place, memories that needed to be put away while he searched for the women. Cole shook his head, forcing the dark thoughts from his mind, and brought the plane in for a soft landing.

He taxied over to the Red Bay's run-down dock, all the while trying to deal with his turbulent emotions. If the women had to spend the night in the wilderness alone, at least it hadn't been on a cold snowy mountaintop like he'd once had to do.

Within seconds of bringing the plane to a stop, Cole saw Jake and his father, Doug, at the top of the hill making their way down to him. He could always count on the good people of Prince of Wales Island to give up their time to look for some lost city folk. Cole unbuckled himself and headed to the rear of the plane. He grabbed his backpack full of medical supplies and his .416 Rigby Magnum rifle.

Prince of Wales Island was black bear country and he didn't know what he'd be up against. In Alaska it was better to be safe than sorry. After loading up with everything he thought he'd need, he opened the hatch of the plane. "I can see you've been keeping up the docks, Jake," he said wryly. Cole realized this would be a wet docking and he needed to go back for his waders.

Doug, Jake's father, was a fisherman by trade and an avid hunter. He always came with everything he needed. "Looks like our Doc Stevens didn't come prepared. Pretty boys always have to look good, don't they, Jakey?" He turned to his son with a big smile on his face.

Jake, who studied the many fish in the Tongass National forest, virtually lived in waders and never thought much of how grubby he looked. His wife,

Sammi, thought he was handsome, though, and that was all that mattered to him.

"Cole?" he said. "Just throw us your stuff and jump. I'll lock up your plane so you won't have to get your fancy mountain gear wet."

"If your dad weren't here right now, I'd give you a lesson in manners, Powell," Cole retorted testily. He threw his bag in Jake's face, took one giant leap and bounded from the plane. Gun held high, he landed on dry land in perfect form.

Jake put the bag down next to Cole and gave him a good swat on the back before he waded out to the plane. "What's got you so ruffled, princess?" He climbed up and locked the plane.

"Jake!" Doug called. "I think Cole's had enough."

"I need to know something," Cole yelled to Jake. "Do you remember when you met your wife, Sammi?"

Jake had just jumped back into the lake. "What are you talking about?" he asked. He looked at Cole as if he was crazy.

Cole donned his backpack and slung his gun around his shoulder. "I'm kind of involved with one of the women who's missing."

Jake waded out of the lake. "Okay, but what does this have to do with my wife? I don't get the connection."

Doug explained. "I think what he's trying to tell you, fish for brains, is that he's fallen for a girl the same way you did for Sammi." He looked at Cole for a denial. When none came he had his answer.

Jake looked at his buddy in shock. "When did you meet her?"

"When I flew up to Marshall's a couple of days ago."

"Is it serious?"

"I don't know," Cole replied. "All I know is that I've never felt this way about a woman before. We were supposed to meet for lunch today. Now…I might be looking for a body." A shadow crossed his face.

"Come on, Cole. Don't go down that road. You and I have saved more people than I can remember. Don't think about your brother. Not today. Think about the people you've saved. So we're looking for a live person now. What's her name?"

"Sashi Hansen. She's up here with her friend Kendra, the other missing girl."

Doug came in and gave him a hug. "Cole, you and Jake are known as miracle workers around here. If anyone can save those girls, it'll be you."

Cole looked up at the brawny man who'd become like a surrogate dad over the years. "Thanks, Doug."

The trio headed up the slope to a clearing a couple of yards from the cabin to obtain their instructions for the search-and-rescue.

Cole caught sight of Jake's twin brother, CJ, also a fire ranger up in the Tongass National Park. It was amazing how alike the two were physically.

Both were tall with dark hair and deep blue eyes, yet each had his own personality. There was, however, one thing they did have in common besides looks. The Powell brothers were brave as hell in situations of life and death.

A hand grabbed him firmly on the arm, and Cole turned to look down at his dear friend Joe Running Bear. He'd never seen Joe look so distressed. "I need you to come with me now, my brother."

Cole sensed Joe wasn't going to leave him alone. "Okay, Joe." He turned to CJ. "I'll catch ya later, pal. Say hi to Natasha for me."

"I will. Good to see you, too, Doc." CJ gave him a big whack on the back.

Cole looked back at the Powells. You could always count on them for love, either in the form of bear hugs from Doug or friendly pummels from the brothers. He envied them for finding themselves such beautiful wives inside and out.

His glance returned to Joe, who packed the same kind of gun Cole carried. When it came to arming themselves on a mission like this, they both thought alike. Now that the search group was assembled, he and Joe made their way to the front of the group to hear instructions from the captain of the Alaska State Troopers.

Trace Hunter stood before the rescuers wearing the brimmed hat and uniform of the police, along with his signature leather duster. "I'd like to thank you for coming out and helping us on our search and rescue today. We have two women last seen by Freddy and some friends at around nineteen hundred hours.

"Our friend Joe Running Bear gave Sashi Hansen a GPS emergency beacon to wear yesterday. It has not been triggered. We hope it still might be used. As I discussed with you, we don't believe the women spent the night at the cabin.

"We're handing out a flyer with the two women's pictures, names and identification. Their families have just been informed. Keep in mind these women are only twenty-eight and both somebody's daughter."

Cole got one of the flyers. His hands shook as he looked at the beautiful picture of Sashi. He read the facts about her: five-four, one hundred pounds, green eyes, strawberry-blond hair.

The other woman was Kendra Knight: five-eleven, 140 pounds, brown eyes and hair.

Cole looked up from his paper to Trace. "It's now thirteen hundred hours. The two women have officially been missing eighteen hours." He began to separate his mind from the task at hand. He was an expert in this field. The most important thing he could do was put his feelings aside and be the search-and-rescue doctor he was acclaimed to be.

"We've divided you into teams," Trace continued, "that will cover the landscape in a distinct pattern so we don't miss anything. Everyone here has an asset. Some of you have ATV's, so you can cover long distances. Some of you have horses, others have dogs. We have four hours till the sun sets. Let's make the most of our time."

"Let's go," Joe said to Cole. "No time to waste."

Joe walked Cole over to where a lone bag lay among the bushes with Native protection charms on it. "This is full of spelunking items to check the caves. I hope we find my friends. I am very worried about them. I think they are going to be near the limestone caves in the area I told them about."

"I'll let you know if that emergency beacon goes off, Joe," Trace said.

"Thank you."

"Good luck."

Cole waved to Trace, who disappeared behind a bush.

A LONE BIRD SANG. THEN IT was joined by others in a cacophony of sounds. Sashi tried to lift her head, but couldn't summon the strength. The birds seemed to mock her in her terrible state of weakness. Did they know she was dying? *Come on, Sashi. Get it together.* She decided to focus on her parents' faces. Her mom's soft brown eyes that shone with joy when she laughed. The safety of her father's arms that made her feel nothing could harm her. She had to fight to stay alive for them.

She closed her eyes and thought how hard she worked for her life. Even if she had not grown up in the wilderness, she knew people like her survived traumatic events like this. She was not going to let her fears get the best of her.

She tried to move her leg, but it was too painful. She must have broken it. If there was a chance she was going to dance again and open her studio, she had to straighten her leg and keep it straight until she received medical care.

The movement was agony. "Oh, God," she gasped. She beat her right hand angrily against her padded vest. It was then she felt the emergency beacon Joe had placed in her pocket the day before.

Gripping the top of her vest with her teeth, she got a strong hold on the zippered pocket and pulled the beacon free with a trembling hand. In tears of anguish, she turned on the signal, praying that somehow her forgetting about the device wouldn't cost Kendra and herself their lives.

She held the beacon to her face and cried, "Please, God, please let someone find me and Kendra. I'll do anything. Please just let us live. Let us be found."

"It's been three hours, Joe. We've searched all known caves and found nothing." Cole was devastated.

"There are other caves, my doctor friend. We just don't know them," Joe said confidently, "but we will continue to search."

Cole watched Joe with his spelunking helmet

on. The man was an odd mix of the modern and the ancient world, but a master tracker. If anyone could find the women, it was Joe.

"Joe? Joe?" Cole heard Trace's voice over the two-way talking device attached to Joe's belt. Joe picked it up. "Roger."

"We've picked up the rescue beacon signal," Trace said. "Do you copy?"

Cole saw Joe begin to shake, saw a tear slide from his jet-black eyes. Both men felt a degree of hope for the first time in three heart wrenching hours of searching. Cole prayed for the women's survival. He knew what it was like to just survive…

"Hold on, Sashi. I'm coming," he whispered to the wind.

"Roger," Joe answered. "Do you have coordinates?"

As he heard the longitude and latitude repeated, Cole triangulated their location on the map. He was shocked to discover they were only a quarter mile away from the beacon's signal. But before they got to the scene, he needed to talk to Trace. Cole was worried about what Joe might see. Even trained first responders had a hard time dealing with the horrors of tragedy.

He walked over and motioned for his friend to hand him the radio.

"Trace, this is Cole."

"Roger that, Stevens."

"Are the Powell brothers in the vicinity?"

"We should be at rendezvous in five minutes. Luck had us mapping that square area of the land when the signal was called in."

"Good to hear. Over and Out."

Cole picked up his belongings and began to head out. "Let's hurry, Joe. If Sashi and Kendra need medical help, I want to reach them as fast as I can."

"I'm with you, my friend." Joe said.

Chapter Four

The sky turned cloudy and it looked as if it might start raining. Dusk was nearly upon them, making Cole nervous about bears, especially as he and Joe approached a dense hemlock forest. Both of them knew the consequences of scaring a bear or coming unaware upon a mother who was protecting her cubs.

He bent down to reach a pocket near the calf of his waterproof hiking pants. He took a bell out of a little rag that held it still and tied it to his belt loop. He was grateful for his Native friend and his insistence on wearing one. He noticed that Joe had done the same thing, except his bell was bigger and hung off his backpack.

Armed with loaded guns, they fought their way through the foliage and emerged into a clearing. Cole's GPS device claimed they were close to the location of the rescue beacon.

The rain forest was coming alive in a new way with owls hooting and vermin scurrying to and fro in the dense underbrush. Cole turned on the light of his helmet for extra help.

Joe began to sing a song in Tlingit. Cole glanced at him and then down the hill at Jake, CJ and Trace. They were taping off an area for police work. That meant they'd found a dead body!

Cole and Joe descended the hill, and Cole looked to the sky while his mind screamed, *Please don't let it be Sashi!* He had to get a grip before he met Jake's eyes. The pair had been in more scrapes and rescues than he could remember. They had a special way of reading each other's body language, which allowed them to converse without speaking.

All Cole had to do was motion to the perimeter. Jake understood immediately and he raised his right hand high then moved it horizontally. Now Cole knew it was the tall woman who was dead, not Sashi. He almost fell over from relief.

He raised his forearms to shoulder height, then let his hands fall open in an outward motion. It was their way of asking how it happened.

Jake spread his hands in the air like bear claws.

"So a bear mauled Kendra," Joe stated, obviously reading Jake's gesture, too.

Cole only nodded. Then he turned away and followed his GPS device until it led him right to a cave. It surprised him to realize he'd passed by this area before, yet had never noticed this cave. The opening was hidden by a large aspen tree that had a big splatter of blood on its trunk.

"Joe? We have something." Cole pointed to the first sign of human existence.

"Captain Powell? We need your help. Do you hear me?"

"Roger that, Cole. I'll be there in a minute. Over and out."

As they drew closer, more blood was noticeable on the bottom of the cave. Joe stayed by Cole's side, and Cole knew the man was keeping his eyes open for any clues one of the women might have left.

Joe threw his pack down and began to call into the cave. "Sashi? Sashi? Are you there? It's Joe!" The old man's voice was filled with concern.

"Stop." Cole took a deep breath. With all his heart he prayed he wouldn't find another mauled body. "Joe, I need you to hurry and unpack our gear. Wait for CJ. I'll go in and survey the first ten feet or so. When he gets here, you two come in after me."

Joe nodded his head in agreement. He sensed why Cole didn't want him to be the first to enter the cave. "I know you will bring her back. You are a great healer." Their eyes met and a chill ran down Cole's spine.

"Be safe, my friend." Cole grabbed Joe's shoulder affectionately.

"Sashi. Sashi Hansen. Can you hear me? It's Cole, the doctor you met a couple of days ago. Dr. Cole Stevens. I'm here to help you." Silence. As he walked into the dank tomblike space, the smell of wet earth filled his nostrils, while fear filled his heart. Was Sashi alive in here?

Grabbing a flashlight out of his backpack, Cole scoured the cave for a clue. When he shone it on the earthen floor, he could see earth had been disturbed. Someone or something had crawled in here recently. That thought got his heart pounding. Her little body could've done that.

The cave ceiling grew lower, forcing him to hunker down while he searched for human life.

"Sashi? Sashi, can you hear me?" He got down on his knees, carefully scanning each side of the dirt crevasses. "It's Cole. Dr. Cole Stevens. Are you there?" Finding strength from within, he kept his voice very calm.

SASHI AWOKE AT THE RUCKUS coming from the opening of the cave. Then a voice permeated her consciousness, making her think she was losing her mind. For how could Cole be here? She must be dreaming. Just then a light ran across the cave. Was this the light people said you walked toward when you were dying?

It was beautiful, she thought. If only she could reach it. She lifted her arm, but she could only make it reach so far before the light fell from her grasp. Was death toying with her?

"Sashi? Sashi, can you hear me?" She heard her name being called in the darkness. In an effort to move her head to the sound, she saw... How could it be? Cole was moving toward her, then seemed to float to the floor beside her.

He grabbed her hands warmly. Tears filled her eyes. She must have done something right to have his beautiful gaze on her again. She was so happy to see him she never wanted him to let go of her. How did he find her?

Cole wouldn't stop talking. He kept saying a name over and over again desperately. She knew it was important to him so she listened intently, and finally her mind connected with the name.

"Sashi," Cole kept saying. He warmed her fingers and looked over her body to see her condition.

She lay there basking in the joy that she'd been found. Cole made her feel so warm and safe. *Sashi,* she thought. *I like that name. It's very pretty. It sounds so familiar. I know a Sashi,* she decided.

She tried to grab Cole's shirt, she was so happy to see him. But she was confused as to what was going on. More tears filled her eyes.

At last she was able to speak. She pulled his hand closer to her body. "What's happened, Cole? Are you a dream? Am I dead?"

"No," Cole replied, his voice calm. "You're alive."

"Then why do you look like an angel?"

HER QUESTION SHOOK HIM to the core. It was at moments like these Cole had to reassure himself that he was the doctor, not the patient. "It's the light on my hat."

"Then why is the light shimmering around your head?" Her voice sounded like sandpaper on wood.

"Sashi, the light helped me find you. It casts a glow around my head so I can see the wounds you've received. Do you remember me telling you I'm a search-and-rescue doctor who flies out to the bush to help people? Well, today I've been searching for you." Cole touched her face with his fingertips, felt the moisture there.

"Cole, I thought you were something I made up to take me to the other side."

Cole gently wiped the tears from her cheeks. "Not today, Sashi. I'm going to do all I can to keep you here. You still owe me a date."

A cough erupted from her beat-up body. Their eyes met and he could see the terror and shock in hers.

He took off his pack and assembled the items he needed.

SASHI HEARD HIM SAY HE WAS grateful she was talking. He began to rattle on about how reviving patients in the bush was a bit trickier. She could tell he was now looking her over like a patient, which made her sad, yet she was still glad he was close. If she wasn't going to die, she knew this man would take care of her.

Cole's voice made her feel more human, more

alive, not one of the dead. She was so grateful for him. He seemed to know exactly what to say and do.

While still holding her hand, he grabbed his stethoscope out of his bag with the other. He listened to her heart and lungs, then finally took her pulse. "It's weak but stable." He flashed her a smile that warmed her from the inside.

"It's a miracle you survived the night, Sashi. When you told me you were a ballerina who worked in the packing plant, I knew you had grit. But you have a mental ability many people don't have. It's hard not to give up in the cold Alaskan night and let fear drive you mad." He caressed her cheek. "But you fought the fear and won."

"Thank you." She tried to give him a smile. He examined the injury on the side of her head without hurting her. Reaching for the penlight on his utility belt, he said, "I have to make sure each pupil is the same size. Those green eyes are perfect, just like I remember."

"What?"

"I'm saying you're in better shape than I expected. My friend Joe Running Bear—"

"There was a giant bear, Cole, and he…" She shuddered in remembered terror.

"I know," he said, "but the bear's gone. You're safe now, Sashi."

"Thank God," she thought she heard him mutter. "Sashi," he said, "I need you to keep hanging on and we'll get you out of here soon."

"Do you know what happened to Kendra? She ran…I tried to stop her…" Sashi was genuinely worried.

Cole held her hand, looked into her eyes and said calmly, "My friends, all dedicated civil servants, are taking care of the search for Kendra. Right now we need to take care of you." The way he talked and cared for her was so warm and gentle.

Sashi had to tell him about Kendra. "Cole… Kendra's pregnant. They need to find her."

Just then she saw Joe quietly entering the cave. "Joe," she said, "any news of Kendra yet?"

Sashi found she could only talk as long as Cole held her hand. He seemed to give her strength, she didn't know why or how.

Joe said, "Sashi, my lone wolf, you are safe and I feel blessed. Believe me when I say Kendra has been found and everything will be okay. You listen to Dr. Cole. He will take care of you."

ONCE JOE HAD CALMED Sashi with his words, Cole whispered to her, "I need to talk to a paramedic just outside the cave." He still hadn't let go of her hand. "I'll be back in two minutes tops and then we'll devise a plan to get you out of here. Joe will be by your side the whole time."

"Promise me you'll be right back?" she begged.

He looked down at the woman he thought had disappeared from his life and squeezed her hand.

"I promise. I just need to get the right equipment to move you, okay?"

"Okay," she murmured.

The look of trust on her face brought back feelings he'd tried to hide, and as he began to slip out of the cave, he struggled against his personal demons. He knew firsthand the trauma she was living through. He'd lived it many nights in his own nightmares. Hard to believe it was twenty years ago that he'd held his dead brother on the mountain after the avalanche, begging him to come back to life. But it wasn't to be. At least today he didn't have to beg God to bring Sashi back.

He had to focus. Right now the only thing important was to get her stable before transporting her. The truth about Kendra could send her into shock. He didn't want anything upsetting her. That was when he changed his mind about leaving her.

He turned back. "Joe?" he said.

"Yeah?"

"Will you please go get Ranger Powell for me? I don't want to leave my patient."

"I'll go now." Joe took off in the darkness.

Cole took a deep breath and leaned over so he could get a closer look at Sashi. Her face was covered with mud and blood. But even that wasn't enough to hide her classic beauty.

Don't lose your focus, Stevens. He had to make sure she was hemodynamic for transportation to a hospital. Amazing she'd survived the night. How many times had they found people who hadn't survived? He didn't envy Trace making the call to Kendra's family.

"New York?" he said to her. "You must lie still so I can examine you thoroughly. All right?"

Her breathing evened out, and she nodded.

Cole felt her neck and began to examine it for spinal cord damage. He couldn't find any. Just in case, he put her neck in a brace to keep it immovable. Later she'd be given an MRI scan and looked over by a radiology team.

Sashi reached for his hand and held on. The strength in those slender fingers surprised the hell out of him.

"Sashi, you're safe," he said.

"I know. You're here now. It's going to be okay."

Cole felt a huge mantle of responsibility as she said those words. He'd always taken his job as a doctor seriously, but in that moment he felt accountable for Sashi. He'd never felt like that before.

He radioed the rescue operation. "Stevens here. I've found Sashi Hansen alive and talking."

"Captain Hunter here. Do you need backup?"

"I've sent out Joe Running Bear to bring in backup." There were audible cheers in the background over the two-way radio. "I need Captain Powell to provide assistance."

He looked at Sashi as he explained the noise over the two-way. "Can you hear that? Everyone is so excited you've been found."

She looked at him and nodded her head. "I just want to leave the cave." She rewarded him with a smile.

"That's what I want, too." He gave her a wink.

"I'm on my way, Cole. Over and out." CJ clicked off.

"I need you to tell me where you hurt the most." He began looking in her ears, mouth, nose and then he pressed on her stomach to check for internal bleeding. She seemed okay.

"Where do you hurt, Sashi?"

Cole examined her left arm, removing the makeshift bandage and looking at the gash. He used his stethoscope to make sure there was still a pulse in the hand. "Can you move your fingers for me?" She wiggled them. She would carry a scar on that arm the rest of her life, but the wound would heal.

"How can I assist?" CJ was in the cave ready to help. Joe was with him.

Relief flooded Cole. CJ Powell had just relocated to Alaska to be a fire ranger and was a newly retired captain from the San Francisco Fire Department. He still kept up on his paramedic skills to aid in search-and-rescue operations. It was just the kind of help Cole needed to get Sashi out of here alive and in good form.

"Sashi, this is one of my best friends, CJ. He's a great paramedic, and you can trust him completely."

"Hello" was all she said.

"CJ, why don't you get over here and help me out with this prima ballerina."

Sashi looked at him seriously. "What if I can never dance again?"

"Sashi, look at me." She did so. "Never stop believing in miracles. You are alive, miracle number one."

"How many miracles are we allowed in this life?"

CJ jumped in. "A lot."

"Isn't that greedy?

"No," Cole said. "I'm a doctor. I see miracles every day."

"Miracles surround us," Joe chimed in. "Just look around. You'll see miracles everywhere. I never stop believing and never should you."

"I'm going to ask you again where you hurt." Cole was more assertive this time.

"My right lower leg," she whispered. "I think it's broken." She was agitated as she looked into Cole's eyes. He saw a flash of determination. He liked that. Despite her condition, she still had spunk.

In one movement they lifted her petite form onto the stretcher. "You didn't survive out here by giving up, Sashi. Don't give up on me now."

While they put blankets on her, Cole told CJ to bandage the injured arm tightly and prepare it for the trip.

"CJ is going to get an IV going. We'll get meds to help with the pain, but I can't do anything until

I've seen all your wounds." Cole had never had a rescue mission where he'd already fallen for his patient. He needed to keep his head clear.

"I've got to look at your leg now. Breathe slowly. One…two…three… All right, let's get a look at that leg. I'm starting at your thigh. Any pain?"

Sashi held on to the sides of the carrier she was on, eyes closed and breathing. "No."

"I now have a hand at your foot and at your knee. I'm going to move your lower leg a little."

"It's tender down there." She whispered through the breaths.

"Let me just check a little bit more. I think you broke your tibia—shin bone. I'm just going to turn it to the…"

Sashi screamed in pain. Then passed out.

IT WAS THE FIRST TIME Cole had sat in the office of the hospital's head psychiatrist. Dr. Daniel Samu-elson had been a great help to Cole, especially with patients who suffered from alcoholism or other ad-dictions. He was also a friend.

"Good to see you, Cole," Daniel said. Cole eyed his distinguished-looking friend. Even though he'd left New York twenty years ago, Daniel still dressed in a suit, or at least a crisp sport jacket and slacks, when he was in the office, something unusual in Ketchikan. His dark hair had been re-cently cut, showing off his handsome tanned face.

He and his wife, Melissa, both in their mid-fifties, traveled whenever they could.

"Thanks for agreeing to meet me," Cole said.

"What's going on?"

"Frankly, I need your help."

His friend gave him a wry smile and took a sip of his coffee. "Is this something I need to be charging for by the hour?"

Cole sat forward. "Possibly."

Daniel got comfy in his chair. "Tell me more."

"I've got a patient. Well, for a variety of reasons she's more than a patient to me." He heaved a troubled sigh. "I need you to help *me* sort out some old issues. But I also need you to help *her*."

Daniel didn't respond right away. At last, looking at Cole intently, he said, "Just so you know, your hour started five minutes ago." He began to write on a pad.

Suddenly Cole felt uncomfortable. This was not the fun guy he usually joked with. This was a different man altogether. "My patient's name is Sashi Hansen. I met her at Marshall's three days before she was going to leave and fly back east. I was up at the resort seeing some sick patients when I met her." Cole looked into the distance.

"Can you explain a little more?"

"I fell for her. I know it sounds crazy, and I realize looks have a lot to do with it, but I swear my feelings are about more than that. I've heard of love at first sight and never believed in it until that redheaded beauty walked into my life. Now everything's complicated."

"*How* is it complicated?"

"I've told you about the time I went helicopter skiing with my brother and an avalanche hit. It killed him instantly and left me alone on the mountain with him for a very cold, lonely night."

Daniel studied him. "How long ago was this?"

"Twenty years."

"What does your brother's death have to do with Sashi?"

Cole put his head in his hands. "Eight days ago I went out on a search-and-rescue mission for two women. They'd been best friends since childhood. One of the women was Sashi Hansen. She survived with serious injuries from a bear attack. Her friend who was ten weeks pregnant was mauled to death. Sashi had put herself in front of the bear to stop it, but her courageous attempt was futile."

Daniel continued to write more information down on his pad. "You weren't kidding about a situation. I heard about it the second I arrived home from Europe. Is Sashi conscious?"

"No, but we're hoping she will be soon. Her body had a bad infection that went systemic. It scared the hell out of me. Only Jake knows my feelings for the patient. I plan on remaining professional until she's healed."

One of Daniel's eyebrows shot up. "That isn't

just your decision to make. Sashi may feel differently. You may risk losing her affection."

"Right now I need to get her better. But I need you to be the one who tells her that Kendra is dead."

"Why can't *you?*" Daniel asked.

Cole shook his head. "I just can't. It brings back too much pain. That's why I've come to you for help."

"I'll help you, but I need to know a few things first. Does she have money to stay here in the hospital? And what about a place to stay afterward?"

Cole shifted restlessly in his chair. "Kendra's parents, the Knights, are very wealthy and are paying all of Sashi's health care costs. And yes, she'll have a place to stay. Sashi's parents are terribly worried about her."

Daniel wrote furiously, then came to a stop. "I'll agree to help as long as you come to group counseling with Sashi."

Cole almost jumped out of his chair. "What?"

Daniel nodded solemnly. "You heard me. I'll help you as long as you help her to know she's not the only person suffering. Group counseling is a wonderful form of therapy that can help you both. *You* need to forgive yourself, too. Survivors guilt is a terrible weight to walk around with."

Cole digested this. "So you'll tell her about Kendra's death and help her?"

"As long as you come to therapy sessions," Daniel stated firmly.

"Deal."

Cole's pager went off. He looked at Daniel. "It's the ICU," he said. "I'll have to use my cell to find out if she's awake now." He dialed the number. "This is Dr. Stevens. I just got a page from your department."

"Dr. Stevens? Dr. Jenkins wanted you to know your patient Ms. Hansen has just awakened and is off the ventilator."

"I'll be right up." Cole clicked off and looked at his colleague. "Do you have time to come with me? I'll pay."

SASHI OPENED HER EYES, but it was hard to focus. She looked around the room and could see she was safe. Where was Cole? He'd promised he wouldn't leave her. And Kendra—where was she? Sashi tried to talk. How long had she been out?

"Help." Her voice came out in a squeak.

"Help." It was worse this time. No sound at all. Her vocal cords didn't seem to want to work. She knew there were buttons to push. She'd seen them on all the shows on TV. There was a red one that should bring somebody. If you needed answers, then who cared if you scared people? At least she was out of that cave.

That's when she found the hospital remote. She pushed the button to call for the nurse, but her bandaged arm hurt like hell. "Can someone help me?" At least she'd found her voice. Sort of.

In just moments it seemed she had a team of doctors and nurses surrounding her. But where was Cole? Where was her family? How come nobody was here? Sure there were flowers. There was even her bedspread from home. Sashi picked it up, wondering how it had got here. Where was her mom?

"Is my family here? Where is Dr. Stevens?"

No one listened. They checked her vitals and told her she was fine. How was she fine? She didn't know them. Oh, that's right. A miracle had happened. She was alive, she hoped she'd be able to dance again...

At that moment Cole strode swiftly through the door in green scrubs. He hadn't forgotten her! He'd saved her and he was still here. He would tell her what was going on.

"Cole!" she said weakly. The nurses had propped her bed up. She could see the man who'd saved her. He had the build of a god. Wow, he was handsome! Even in a delusional state she could tell that. She was so happy to see him, to see somebody she knew. He hurried to her bed.

COLE CAUGHT HIMSELF. All he wanted to do was kiss the woman senseless and tell her how happy he was that she was alive. But the best thing for her right now was the care of a doctor. Also a friend. That's what he was going to be.

He gave her a warm smile. "New York, you're truly our miracle patient."

"I am?"

He nodded. "You gave us all a scare. You were rushed into surgery for the tibial fracture on your leg and reconstructive surgery on your arm. Those surgeries went well—until you had a pneumothorax emergency."

"I don't understand," she said, obviously confused. He could tell she wanted more from him, but he refused to show any emotion.

"It means your lungs were going to collapse."

"Oh, dear."

"Don't worry. You're doing much better."

"Can you tell me about my leg? Will I dance again?" Sashi looked at him with hope.

He turned to glance at Daniel for support, gripping his hands together to keep them from touching her. "Yes. You had one of the more fortunate kinds of leg break. You'll need to be on crutches for the next eight weeks, but with two to four months of rehab, you should be dancing again."

Sashi awoke again to a hospital room filled with flowers. An older man wearing a white doctor's jacket over a suit stood up and walked over to her. Cole stayed in the background. "Hello, Ms. Hansen. I'm Dr. Samuelson." He extended his hand and she shook it. He had a very firm handshake.

"Dr. Stevens and I have worked very hard on your case and we'd been waiting for you to wake up. In fact he had a pager that alerted him the moment you did. That's how he was able to get here so fast."

She smiled at Cole. "Thank you," she said before turning her attention back to the older doctor. Sashi liked the soothing quality of his voice. It had a familiar ring, too. "I guess you're from Brooklyn."

"No, from Queens, but close," he said with a laugh. "Not many people in this part of the country can guess my hometown. Where did you live?"

"In Manhattan at the Joffrey Ballet School, then moved to the Village with six other girls all trying to make it big."

"Did you make it big?"

"Would I be here if I had?"

"That depends on your conception of making it big. Many girls would give anything just to be accepted to that school. You have to tell me what you consider 'making it big.'"

Sashi's head started to reel. "Can...can you tell me what day it is?"

"Ah...now you want to start talking about reality."

She looked at Cole. "Could you tell me if my mother is around? The blanket from my bedroom is here, but I don't see her or my friend Kendra. Where is she? Joe said everything would be all right."

The two doctors exchanged glances. The silence allowed her to give voice to her fears, the premonition she'd had all along. Tears began to course

down her cheeks. "No…no, she can't be!" Her body
became racked with sobs. "How can my best friend
be gone?"

The older man handed her the tissue box that
was next to her bed. She grabbed several tissues
and hid her face behind them. "I tried to stop the
bear, but Kendra took off then climbed a tree. I
couldn't stop the bear."

Cole came over and sat down on the bed. He
took her hand, clearly trying to comfort her.

The other doctor sat down in the nearest chair.
"Sashi," he began, "I want to tell you a story."

"Why? What story?" Sashi struggled to stop
crying.

"This is a good story. I think it will help you.
Early on in my practice a young man brought in a
picture of his family—his wife and three beautiful
children. He showed me the picture and I agreed
he had a lovely family. Then he asked me a question. It was one of the hardest questions I'd ever
been asked in all the years I'd practiced psychiatry."

Sashi's heart was pounding. She was terrified
of what this doctor had to tell her. "What was the
question?"

"He asked me how come he was still alive when
they're all dead?"

Sashi reached for Cole's hand and squeezed it.
"How did the family die?"

"I believe they were all in a car accident. But
the real question here is how come he's still alive?"

Sashi's eyes watered. "I don't know."

"I was baffled, too. I went and asked a dear friend and colleague of mine the same question. You know what he said?"

Sashi just blinked.

"He said, 'Ah! The young man hasn't yet figured out the joy that he's still alive!'"

"I get it," Sashi said, her voice cracking. "You want me to find joy in why I'm alive."

"Yes."

Sashi couldn't speak for a moment. At last she asked, "How did Kendra die?"

"The bear killed her, probably at the very moment you were able to escape into the cave," Cole answered.

Sashi couldn't stop her gut-wrenching cry. She reached out to Cole and his arms drew her into an embrace. She sobbed on his shoulder. He held her tenderly, saying nothing more. He just gave her tissues and rocked her gently.

When Sashi was finally able to speak again, she didn't dare move from her cocoon. "How long was I asleep here?"

Dr. Samuelson answered. "Eight days."

"How could I have been out for so long?" she mumbled against Cole's sleeve.

"You had a cut on your back that got infected," Cole replied. "It was touch and go for a while. I blame myself for not checking you out better. I'm sorry I didn't do a thorough job of taking care of you." His voice sounded shaky.

Sashi looked up from his loving embrace and saw his pain. "Why are you apologizing to me? You saved my life. Don't ever apologize to me again. I don't think I even recall getting a cut on my back. My leg and arm hurt so badly, I don't remember feeling pain there."

"It doesn't matter. I should've been more meticulous."

"Stop it. You saved my life. You were the angel who came and rescued me." She reached up and touched his face. Their eyes met and she almost kissed him, but Cole started to ease himself away. She felt a little wounded by his retreat.

"A lot has happened while you've been asleep," he said.

"Tell me."

"Well, the Knights are taking care of all your medical expenses."

"That sounds like something they would do." A sob escaped. "I just can't believe Kendra's gone."

Dr. Samuelson stepped in. "Sashi, we're going to leave now. You need rest. And I think it would be a good idea to call your mom. You should talk to her."

Cole reached down and handed Sashi the blanket. "Your family sent you this to remind you of home. I've heard that they've called hourly, just waiting for you to come around. They wanted you to phone them as soon as you did."

"I will." She stared at Cole. "I need to thank the Knights for all their help, but I don't know how I can talk to them after what's happened to Kendra."

"You have to remember that you lived," Dr. Samuelson interjected. "You tried to save their daughter. People don't give their money away freely. They must love you dearly. This is a gift. You need to start seeing your survival as a second chance at life. As soon as you're well enough I'm going to have you come to group therapy to begin the healing process and deal with your feelings of guilt."

"But how…?"

"One hour, one day at a time."

Sashi wondered how she could ever be a whole person again after losing her best friend. And what did it all mean for her and Cole? Would he ever feel for her the same way? Or was he going to just be a doctor to her now?

Chapter Five

Cole eyed her with concern. "Just so you know, my friend Jake, who's the head ranger, and another buddy of mine, Trace Hunter, the captain of the Alaska State Troopers, tracked the bear and put it down. The cubs have been taken to a zoo in Canada. I hope that will bring you some peace."

Sashi shook her head. "Maybe it will bring peace to Kendra's family. We messed up, Cole. Broke all the rules about safety in the wild. I just wish…" Her words trailed off.

"No amount of wishing is going to change the situation. You have to learn to be grateful for the life you have." He could see the confusion on her beautiful face. All he wanted to do was hug and comfort her.

"So how long am I going to be in here?" Sashi asked, sniffling.

"Maybe a week or two, and then you'll have your own little apartment. In a couple of weeks we'll have you come back here for daily rehab sessions and group therapy with Dr. Samuelson, here." The best part of all this, Cole thought, was that Sashi would not be returning home so quickly.

"How will I get around? Is there a bus service?"

"A couple of times a week, when you'll be in group therapy with Dr. Samuelson, I'll bring you to the hospital with me. On the days you don't have group therapy, you'll take a cab to the hospital for physical therapy. Your therapist, Mary Brown, will take you home. She'll also help clean the place and cook dinner. Mary is Joe Running Bear's daughter."

"How is this all possible?" Sashi asked, her brow furrowed. "It doesn't make sense. I can't afford it."

"No, you can't," Daniel replied. "But if you take the help from the Knights, from Mary and from others who are willing to assist you, you'll get the care and treatment you need and deserve. One day you'll be able to dance again. If you were to go home now, would you be able to get that kind of care?"

"You doctors already know the answer to that question," she said, "but I've never been the type to let anyone take care of me. It's very hard. How come my parents haven't come here?"

"I believe your parents are saving their money to fly out and pick you up once you're better."

Daniel stood up. "I'll leave now so that you can call your mom and dad. Then you need to get a good night's sleep. Once your phone call's done, the nurse will give you something to help you sleep."

"It's been good talking to you, Doctor."

"See you soon, Sashi." He turned and left.

SASHI LOOKED AT COLE. "Please don't go till I'm asleep. I've got to call my parents."

He handed her a cell phone, then sat in a chair close to the bed. She punched in the numbers she'd known since she was a child and heard her father's voice. "Daddy—I've missed you so much."

"We want to see you, baby," he said. "Tell me and we'll be on the next flight out, which we've wanted to do all along. But since we heard they're holding off burying Kendra till the autopsy is completed, we're debating between coming while you're healing or when you're better. When do you think you'll need us most?"

"Oh, Dad, I always need you and Mom, but I guess you know the Knights are helping me out financially."

"Is that my little girl I hear on the phone?" said Sashi's mother.

Hearing her mother brought tears to Sashi's eyes. "I got my blanket, Mom. I miss you so much and wish you were here. But they have an incredible staff here and I'm going to need you more when the real healing starts."

"Did you know I talked to you for hours and hours while you were in the coma? The Knights paid the long distance bill. And we've spoken to your doctor, Cole Stevens. We understand that he's the doctor who saved your life. He must be pretty special."

"He's a great doctor, Mom, but can we talk about him later?"

"So he's there with you in your room right now." Her mom paused. "That's good."

"Yeah. Mom, they gave me some medicine and I'm starting to fall asleep, so I better let you go. Love you."

COLE TOOK THE PHONE and turned it off. Then he lowered her bed to a flat position. Sashi's eyes were closing and he could see she was falling asleep. He needed to leave the room and go home. As he walked to the door, he looked back at Sashi who, despite her pallor, was utterly beautiful, her gorgeous red hair something he would love to get lost in.

You need to take a breather, pal, he told himself. He'd walked such a tightrope since he'd found her on the cave floor. It was an enormous relief to know she hadn't died and would recover. The most important thing now was to help her recover *mentally* after such a traumatic event.

No matter how much he liked Sashi, he refused to take advantage of her while she was in such a weak state. Since she was stuck up here in Alaska with no family or friends, he would be the doctor she could trust. He'd be a friend, *not* a boyfriend at the beginning of a blooming relationship. The promise did not make him particularly happy, but it was the right thing to do.

IT HAD BEEN THREE DAYS since Sashi had seen Cole and she missed him. But he could be out on a rescue or simply have the time off. She was nervous and excited to see him again. What was it going to be like? Now that their relationship had changed so much, Cole was her doctor and the man who'd saved her life.

Not only had she fallen for him that night beneath the stars when they had kissed so intimately, but now he had become her lifeline here in Ketchikan. How was she going to behave with him? She didn't know what to do. What did a person in her circumstances do? All she could do was follow her gut instincts and hope they led her in the right direction.

To pass the two hours until her first group therapy session, Sashi found a rerun on TV that kept her entertained. The show was *So You Think You Can Dance.* She'd heard about the series, but never had time to see it. Now she could see why some of her friends enjoyed it. The dance sets were incredibly well choreographed.

Sashi sipped on water and glanced at the clock. She wondered what the group therapy session would be like. She'd never gone to a psychiatrist before. There was a part of her that didn't want to go at all. Yet, the horror of what she'd lived through and the loss of her best friend continued to haunt her daily and in her dreams.

All she thought about was how she should have, *could* have done more to save Kendra. She felt entirely undeserving of the Knights' generosity.

One thing she definitely wanted to do was find Freddy and give him a piece of her mind. If he'd acted like a man, Kendra would never have run from the cabin. She would still be alive with his child. *That bastard.*

She seemed to leap from sorrow to hate at a moment's notice.

She missed Kendra so much. Her friend would've known exactly what to say to cheer her up.

She needed to get herself together. Sashi was grateful Joe had brought her suitcases to the hospital. It was nice to wear her own clothes. One of the nurses had dressed her in a comfortable dress for the day and put her in a wheelchair.

Sashi waved to the nurses on her floor as she wheeled herself through the hospital corridor. As the door opened she backed herself in, hitting the button for level four, the "crazy" ward as she liked to call it.

She pushed the handicap button to back herself into the room. After wheeling around, she just about fell out of her chair when she saw who was sitting opposite Dr. Samuelson.

COLE WAS ELATED TO SEE Sashi come through those doors. Over the past few days he'd had to go out with Jake and find some hikers lost in the Misty Fjords. He'd radioed in to the hospital to see how Sashi was doing. It was a known fact that when someone was as physically fit as she was, the ability to regain strength and heal was greater. So he wasn't surprised to learn about her amazing progress.

Except that nothing beat seeing the real thing. Sashi Hansen was in her full glory, getting her sass back. She wore a floral print dress that hugged her chest in a way that made his heart pound. He took in the rest of her. The sleeves left room for bandages. The dress came to her knees and of course her one foot had the boot she'd be wearing for another seven weeks.

But the other foot had a shoe with a little flair, a dainty flat covered in silver sequins. And her hair—the glorious red tresses seemed shot with gold as they tumbled over her shoulders. And as she wheeled closer to him, he noticed her lovely eyes—greener than he remembered them being. God, she was beautiful.

His heart beat furiously.

He had to remind himself that she needed a doctor and a friend who was in control and professional. *You've got to let her heal before she knows how you feel.*

"YOU'RE HERE!" SHE EXCLAIMED with joy. "But why? I don't understand."

He looked happy. "I'm here for group therapy."

"What?" She felt as though she was going crazy. "You mean the group is just the two of us?"

"Yes." Sashi looked at him more closely to see if he was telling the truth, but she shouldn't have. His tanned face was more handsome than ever, and his shirt and jeans showed off his broad shoulders and muscular thighs. It seemed every time she saw him there was something new. Like how sexy he looked when he put his hand on his neck, causing his biceps to bulge, and met her gaze. It was enough to make her weak at the knees. Thank heaven she was sitting.

At last she averted her eyes, not wanting to look at him anymore. Until she figured out what was going on between them, she decided she needed to focus on her recovery and not her heart.

She closed her eyes, fighting for composure. She was here to heal. All they'd shared was a night of kissing, and then he'd rescued her. Now he was her doctor. "I may not understand, but I'll roll with it." She turned her attention to Dr. Samuelson. She'd already done some therapy with him this week, and she trusted him.

The psychiatrist stood up and walked up to the chalkboard. He wrote, "Survivors Guilt," then returned to his seat. "Sashi and Cole, I'm glad you're both here. Each of you has survived a very traumatic event. We're going to do a variety of exercises to help you cope with the pain you're suffering now."

Sashi turned to Cole in shock. "Is he serious? Have you been through something terrible, too?" She immediately felt a new connection with Cole.

Cole brought his chair closer to Sashi's. "Yes," he said. "I once lived through a nightmare." Their eyes met in mutual pain. Sashi was barely aware that she'd grabbed his hand. "I'm sorry," she whispered.

"Cole's about to start a process that's very difficult," Dr. Samuelson said. "He's going to try to tell us how exactly his trauma occurred. He brought in a picture to share, in order to recreate the scene. Cole? We're ready when you are."

HE DIDN'T REALIZE HOW MUCH he needed Sashi's strength until she grasped his hand. They both had suffered and soon she would know what he'd done to his brother.

From a back pocket he pulled out his wallet, then flipped it open to a picture of two handsome teenage boys standing on their skis next to a helicopter.

Sashi leaned closer. "Are you the shorter one?"

Cole turned to her in surprise. "How did you know?"

"It's your eyes and the way you hold yourself. Is that your brother? He looks just like you."

"Yeah, that was my older brother, Luke. We

were two years apart but pretty much inseparable. We were ski racers who traveled the world racing. When we weren't racing, we were training in South America, New Zealand and on the glaciers of Europe and Oregon."

"Wasn't that dangerous?" Daniel asked.

"Sure, but we weren't scared of anything, especially Luke. We loved coming back home to Alaska and skiing up in the Chugach. Nothing beat heli-skiing on fresh powder."

"Tell us what happened," Daniel encouraged him.

Cole began to rub Sashi's hand almost like a worry stone. "I was heli-skiing with Luke where we grew up in Valdez. It was a perfect snow day and Luke was one of the best skiers in the world. The family thought he was going to make the Olympics that year. He jumped first. I followed him.

"The powder was shoulder deep and the air crisp with the scent of pine. With a sun shining above us, it was heaven. We laughed as we crisscrossed down hundreds of vertical feet of snow, until we came to a chute where we both stopped. It was a gnarly one, and only the craziest of crazy skiers would ever go on it.

"I said to Luke, 'The trials are only a week away. Let's play it safe, bro.' But he never played it safe. My heart pounded so hard I thought it was going to burst. I had a dreadful feeling and screamed, 'Don't!'

"He jumped into that chute like he was born to ski it. But the last storm had turned the snow to ice underneath the powder. It gave way and Luke was sucked in like a vacuum. He was wearing a beacon. I jumped down to the other side of the chute and chased that damn avalanche, praying I would get to him in time to dig him out.

"I did get to him and started digging, but the snow gave way. I fell another hundred feet, sliding down the mountain till a tree stopped me. I broke my left leg in a place similar to your break, Sashi. All I could do was drag myself back to Luke.

"Night was coming, but I didn't care. I just kept praying that the helicopters passing over would stop and help. Then a storm set in. I made it back to where Luke was. He'd been dead for how long I don't know. I dug us a snow cave and prayed all night that God would bring my brother back.

"The next day rescuers found us. Even though I knew Luke was gone, I still hoped they could save him somehow. This is where you come in, Sashi. When I heard you talking in the cave and saw your face, I related to you on a level I never had with anyone before."

SASHI WAS STUNNED BY what she'd heard. She couldn't believe the man who'd rescued her and was now a doctor had undergone something so tragic.

She shook her head. "How did you find the strength to go on living? You're like a superhero.

To think you're a doctor who goes out in a bush plane and rescues people..." Knowing this about Cole made her do some self-checking. She realized that dreams don't have to be discarded.

He'd lost a brother and had turned it into something noble. She'd been told she could dance again, so there was no reason to think she wouldn't be able to open her studio.

"Cole," Dr. Samuelson said, "do you find that you push yourself harder and harder to fight depression and anxiety? Do you think you picked the field of medicine you did to prove to your brother over and over again that you didn't mean to let him die on the mountain?"

Cole looked at the doctor and finally nodded. "Every time I'm out there on a rescue, I try to prove that I beat the odds and can make it right this time. The day Luke died, I gave up ski racing and focused on school. With my injury, I couldn't ski anyway, and I found out I was actually pretty smart. I used my brains to get into medical school and then to service."

Sashi looked at him. "Have you forgiven yourself yet? To me it sounds like you did everything you could to save your brother. And over the years you've done so much to help others, your brother would be proud."

His eyes watered. "I don't think I'll ever forgive myself. I think you know the feeling."

Tears filled her eyes, too, and she nodded. "I

know it all right. But your brother died twenty years ago. At some point you *have* to forgive yourself. You did nothing wrong."

"Neither did you," Cole responded.

At that, she brushed her tears away, and the gesture made him reach for her. He lifted her out of the wheelchair—she was so small, it was easy to sweep her up in one swift movement—and wrapped his arms around her. Here was one person who truly understood his suffering.

Sashi's sweet body and her kindness released his emotions. It felt so right to have her in his arms while he let go of twenty years of sorrow.

"Cole," Daniel interjected, "Sashi's right, you know. Over the next sessions we're going to learn how to forgive ourselves and move on. We understand it's okay to be sad for the loss of our loved one, but we can't blame ourselves for that loss. It was just a freak accident."

"Daniel, I hear what you're saying." Cole had been playing with Sashi's incredible hair, inhaling her sweet fragrance. "But how do I forgive myself when I know my parents haven't truly forgiven me?"

"Put Sashi back in the chair—or at least look at me."

Cole didn't want to let her go. Instead, he tucked her into his neck. Cole had had no idea how weak he was until this moment. He hadn't been ready to talk about any of this. But now he was willing to do it for this redheaded beauty he'd fallen in love with.

"Are you sure they haven't forgiven you?" Daniel said. "Or are you walking around with extra guilt you've put on yourself."

Cole met Daniel's gaze. "That's a very good question."

Daniel glanced at his watch. "Our session is over for today. Sashi, next time it's going to be your turn to share your story."

She pulled away to look up at Cole, and knew she could do it now that she had Cole by her side. For the first time since the cave, Sashi saw more than friendship in his eyes. She was confused, but so happy to be safe and secure in his arms.

Cole smiled. "It'll be okay. I'll be here." Then he pulled her close again, letting her know that he meant what he'd said.

Chapter Six

It was late afternoon.

Sashi sat nervously on her bed waiting for Cole to help finish getting her discharged. She knew this day had to come where she would be leaving the comforts of the hospital and living on her own until she was going to fly home. Admittedly she'd been assured the small apartment was close to Cole's house and her new physical therapist, but the knowledge didn't allay her fear.

The thought of being alone at night terrified her. The nightmares and panic attacks hadn't abated with therapy. She'd been seeing Dr. Samuelson privately for the past week. He was going to send her home with various prescriptions to help with those problems. She was going to take the pills for a little while to see if they helped, but her goal was to get off them as soon as possible.

Now she was going to be on her own, alone in a foreign place, using crutches or a walker to get around. If she fell, she would get up just as she'd been taught in physical therapy. A fierce dancer, she'd fallen countless times. She wasn't going to stop moving or let fear stop her. First, at her therapist's suggestion, she would always wear clothes with pockets so she could carry a cell phone with her at all times. Second, she would refuse to cry or feel sorry for herself.

Hard to believe it had been over three weeks since she'd been admitted to the hospital. With the help of Joe's daughter, Mary Brown, a truly gifted physical therapist, she was able to rely on a walking cast and without a wheelchair. It comforted her to know that both Cole and Mary didn't live far away.

"New York, you ready to get out of here?" Cole came into her room with a wheelchair. He was wearing fitted charcoal pants with a pale gray sweater, and his flaxen hair was still damp from a shower.

Sashi swallowed hard as she took in the sight of this amazing man. She didn't know what was going to happen between the two of them. They lived such different lives, had such different dreams.

Yet they had a powerful bond. Both had lost a loved one and both felt responsible for the loss. Both were now in therapy helping each other get over their respective guilt. When it came to daily interaction, Cole acted as if she was an acquaintance. Someone he was merely friends with. She was learning, too, to cope with his change of moods; one day he would act as if he adored her, and the next he'd act like merely a friend. And if they *were* going to be only friends, she knew it was good he was distancing himself.

Her problem was telling her heart that she had to get over him, which was near to impossible with him around all the time. Hopefully, now that she was no longer in the hospital, she wouldn't see him as much and maybe that would help. "I'm ready as I'll ever be!"

COLE SURVEYED THE HOSPITAL room he'd come to think of as his second home, then turned his gaze to Sashi. She was coming back to life. She had color in her cheeks, a tad more weight on her bones and she smiled more. Her hair shone, and a green sweater dress set off her beautiful face and hugged her body, showing off her lithe dancer's figure. He gulped in reaction, wondering how he was going to leave her alone. He looked back at her face and her lovely eyes, eyes that sparkled like emeralds.

He could feel his body tighten in response, but he knew she needed a friend now, not a lover.

"You look beautiful," he said. *Way to go, Stevens. Way to keep it friendly.*

She looked startled. "Thanks. Mary got me this dress and a few other clothes since most of my clothes were only fit for Marshall's Resort."

"Mary's amazing."

"Yeah."

"So shall we get you out of here and settled into your new place?"

Cole watched her stand up with the aid of the walker and hop over to the wheelchair he held for her. He had to hide the disappointment he felt at not being required to pick her up and put her in the wheelchair. But for her sake he was thrilled she was becoming independent.

SASHI FELT SELF-CONSCIOUS being wheeled through the hospital by Cole. She could hear doctors and mostly nurses all saying "Hi" to Cole. Who could blame them? He was a catch and the lucky woman who won his heart… She would have to stop thinking about that.

They made a quick stop at the hospital pharmacy to pick up her meds.

"Do I really need all of this?" Sashi was shocked at the size of the bag.

"For now, yes."

"All right." She hated being so dependent on Cole. Surely it was a burden for him. But then, after what she'd learned from his past, she knew the reason he'd taken the Hippocratic oath to the extreme. He felt a connection to her and wanted to make sure she was safe and protected until she could return home. Until then, he was one of the only people she knew out here in Alaska.

She was grateful for his help as a doctor, and

hopefully she would heal soon so both she and Cole could get back to their lives.

After waiting to be discharged and get her medicine, she and Cole walked out into a dark, foggy night. Sashi hadn't realized how late it had gotten. "I love that pungent smell of pine," she said. "I've missed being outside."

"But it's such a cold, foggy night." Cole sounded surprised.

She looked up at his striking profile. "I know it sounds shocking. A city girl like me falling in love with the wonders of Alaska. It's almost unheard of." Sashi looked away quickly so he wouldn't think he was one of the wonders.

"All right, Miss Alaska. Let's get you out of the cold and into my car. It's just over here."

She could see where they were headed. He owned a sleek, black Range Rover. The car definitely suited him. He seemed to be one of those people who fit in wherever he went. It was that magnetic personality—he drew people to him. He went ahead and started the car, then came to get her, always Mr. Thoughtful.

Cole opened the passenger door for her. Before she could grab her walker or crutches, he picked her up in his arms. It caused a flurry of sensations she tried to tamp down. "Will you put your arm around my neck while I get you settled in the car?" he said. "I don't want to drop you."

When she did as he asked, her head turned and

her cheek brushed against his. She felt a jolt of electricity and sensed he felt it, too. But maybe it was just her imagination.

"Thanks for all your help," she said coolly. "You've gone beyond the call of duty to help a patient." The moment was broken, but she knew she was right. The sooner she started acting like a patient and not a potential lover, the sooner she would get over Cole.

He set her into the plush leather passenger seat. The glance he gave her caused her belly to fill with butterflies. She immediately forced her gaze in front of her and pretended she hadn't noticed. Cole closed the door and proceeded to load her belongings into the trunk.

COLE WAS RATTLED. HAD SASHI really fallen in love with Alaska? She wasn't a woman to mince words. How could she have anything but terrible memories of this state after what had happened to her and Kendra?

He'd been so consumed with helping Sashi get better so she could live her dream of opening her own dance studio. Unfortunately he'd never once stopped to ask her what else was going on in her mind. He'd made assumptions—but perhaps the wrong assumptions. This was something he needed to discuss with Daniel.

At last he climbed into the driver's seat and turned up the heat. "Aren't you cold?"

She shrugged. "I'm okay. I got used to being cold most of the time while I lived in the bunk-house Marshall's provided. It was nothing like what the clientele stayed in. And as for the showers and toilets, let's just say I felt like I was a lumberjack this summer."

Cole laughed as he steered the car through the streets of the sleepy town. "I've heard stories about the conditions up there at Marshall's, but never heard them put so…politely." He toggled through some buttons on the dash. Pretty soon she heard a tune with a great reggae beat.

Sashi grinned. "You probably heard the conditions are just plain shitty."

His laughter again echoed in the car, and it was the kind of laughter she hadn't heard since the first time she met him. "That's getting a little bit closer to what I've heard. Then you worked in the pit of hell cutting up fish. I hope you made enough money to open your studio."

"I did. I couldn't believe it when I got my check. I wired the money home that very day since Kendra and I were going to be traveling a little. Hopefully it will be enough for me to get my loan," she said with excitement. "I want to teach children ballet."

"That's wonderful."

"Hey," she said, gesturing to the radio, "this is great music. Who is it? I've never heard it before. Sounds like music that belongs in the Caribbean, not up here in Alaska."

"You don't know?" he said. "You make me feel like an old man. How old are you, anyway?"

"Didn't you look on my chart? Everyone else asked me my date of birth every other second."

"Yes, I looked. I'm a good seven years older than you."

Sashi wrinkled her nose. "Why does it matter if friends are seven years apart in age? You've been so kind to me. I can't thank you enough." In a more serious voice she added, "And as my doctor, you've been the best."

Kind...doctor...the best. Damn. He'd played his role so well, she really believed he had no romantic interest in her. She believed he'd taken pity on her and was simply taking care of her. If only she knew what was going on in his head!

This was an impossible situation. He didn't know what was right or wrong anymore now that she was out of the hospital. She was getting better, but the time still didn't seem right to let her know how he felt. Sashi was still too vulnerable.

"You haven't told me the name of the group we're listening to," she reminded him.

"It's UB40. I grew up with a lot of their music. Like I said, I'm an old man."

"That's ridiculous. I don't think of you as old at all. And for the record, I like this music a lot."

"Will you tell Jake that?" Cole flashed her a smile to hide what he was really thinking.

"Sure. Why?"

"Jake thinks the only good music is eighties rock."

"I think you two sound like a pair. I'd like to meet him one day."

"That should be easy to arrange."

SASHI HADN'T REALIZED how fast they'd climbed out of Ketchikan proper until she saw lights popping out of the fog. "Where's the apartment I'm going to be staying in?"

"It's actually right around the corner." They took a hairpin turn and she could see trees and lush green shrubbery poking through the fog. Also a big wood-sided house came into view. He pushed a button on a remote, and the garage door opened. He pulled into an enormous space—she saw a speed boat on one side along with a Porsche and tons of sporting equipment.

Perplexed, she asked, "Do I live in this person's house?"

"You'll stay in the mother-in-law apartment. It's located on the main level."

"Do you know the owner of this house?" She wrung her hands. "Are they trustworthy?"

"I know him and he's very trustworthy, but you'll have to make that decision yourself."

Sashi was getting annoyed at the game. "Who is he?"

Cole flashed her a crooked smile. "It's me. Did you think I'd let you go recuperate anywhere? Joe owns some property up the road. His daughter and son-in-law have built a home on it while he lives in a trailer out back. Mary comes down and helps me keep this place clean and cooks some meals, so I don't live just on energy bars."

"You sound like me. I forget to eat half the time." She laughed. "It's also a great way to eat on the cheap."

He slipped briefly into doctor mode. "I'm thinking it's a low-calorie way for a dancer to eat."

"Hey, I'm naturally skinny. And living in the Big Apple is pricey, Doc."

"I'm watching you, New York."

She eyed him seriously. "Go ahead! My parents are amazed at what this body can pound."

"Listen, Mary and Joe want you to know you can always stay with them when I can't be here. Joe adores you. I think if he were younger, he might take you for a wife."

"Now you're teasing me—Joe only likes Tlingit women." She twisted in the seat to face him. "How could you have kept all these plans a secret from me?"

She felt hurt that he hadn't trusted her enough to tell her, and she didn't know how she was going to get over her feelings for him when she'd be living in such close proximity to him.

"Come on, Sashi. I couldn't go around the hospital and announce I'm having you live with me. It wouldn't sound good. But I have a surprise for you inside the house, so cheer up. You're out of that hospital now. Let's go in and celebrate."

Cole opened her door and carefully picked her up. Sashi put her arms around his neck, savoring the feel of being warm and protected. She couldn't believe how relieved she was that she was going to be staying with him. No matter what kind of relationship they had, at least he wasn't leaving her alone in Alaska.

She rested her head against his neck. All her anxieties were slipping away. In fact, she was beginning to feel sleepy. Cole opened the door with ease as he carried her into the dark house.

From out of nowhere she heard a whisper, then, "Welcome home, Sashi!" The lights came on and she looked around to see at least twenty people in Cole's living room. Surprised, she instinctively clung more tightly to Cole.

He looked down at her. "Welcome home, New York. Since you don't have your family, I thought I'd invite mine over to welcome you." The joy on his face was so genuine, it made her heart soar.

"Thank you," she whispered in his ear. She then turned her head and surveyed the room. "Joe, Mary, Mac…. I'm afraid I don't know the rest of you. But I want to thank all of you for coming here to welcome me. It means a lot." Her eyes began to tear up.

The room erupted with voices all talking at once. "We're happy you're better and home from the hospital," Joe said.

Cole jumped in. "Thanks, everyone, for helping make Sashi's release from the hospital so special. I love you all." The room erupted in cheers. He carried her over to a plush leather couch with an ottoman and set her down. Then he sat right next to her.

His house was absolutely beautiful, she thought. It was all one floor except it had a loft with a polished light wood balcony and stairs that led up to it rising from the back of the home.

His open-concept kitchen was a focal point of the place, with a bark-colored granite slab bar running the length of the room. The whitewashed custom cabinets had intricate wood carvings. Stainless-steel Sub-Zero appliances were the jewels that put the finishing touches on the majestic room.

Set off to the right was a magnificent dining room with a large window she assumed must look out over the woods surrounding the house. The carved dining room table was a piece of art in itself.

The living room was square with leather couches surrounding a stunning fireplace. In a space off the living room was a U-shaped couch in black leather facing a theater type screen surrounded by built-in cabinets, and a little farther back, off in a corner, was a pool table. Definitely a bachelor pad. Lacquered wood reached to a pitched roof twenty feet above. Beams spanning each room throughout the house met in the living room, adding elegance. All the floors were done in high-sheen hardwood, accented with various types of small rugs, some bearskins, others intricately woven Native rugs. She wondered where her apartment was.

A man came over who looked like CJ, the paramedic who'd helped her in the cave. Except he had a certain ruggedness CJ lacked. "I've got a surprise for you." He went to the stereo and put on a song.

Cole bent down and whispered in her ear, "Jake's been dying to do this." Suddenly she realized that Jake and CJ were twins! In a moment the house was booming with Jay-Z's "Empire State of Mind" featuring Alicia Keys.

Jake pulled up a chair next to her. "I wanted to play a song for the girl who goes by the nickname New York. I thought it would make you feel more at home."

"Oh, I definitely love this song." Sashi gestured to several cute little girls across the room dancing to the beat. "Who are they?"

Cole reached for the remote to his stereo and turned the music down a little. Jake nodded in the direction of the girls. "The little blonde falling over is my daughter, Christina, and the—"

"—dark-haired dancer is my beautiful granddaughter, Abigail," Joe broke in. "She's a wonderful dancer, just like her mom." He was sitting on the other side of the couch.

Mary was play-dancing with her daughter. Sashi called over to her. "I didn't know you danced. Why didn't you tell me?"

"It wasn't the right time. Soon I'll tell you many things."

Sashi took in a deep breath and turned to Joe. "Do you and your daughter always speak so cryptically?"

"I can answer that. Yes." A pleasant-looking man in his late thirties with curly blond hair shook Sashi's hand before sitting down beside Joe. "I'm Eric Price, Mary's husband and Joe's son-in-law." He wrapped his arm around Joe.

"See, Sashi?" Joe said. "I raise my daughter in the ways of the Tlingit, and I get a white man for a son. But then he gave me my Abigail and now life is good. She is a daughter of the raven, like her grandma."

Sashi smiled at him. "It's so good to see you, Joe."

"Not as good as it is to see you, my little wolf."

"Please, no talk of that tonight."

Joe shook his head. "Another time."

Jake led a small group of people Sashi didn't recognize over to her. "Sashi, I'd like to introduce you to my wife, Sammi. She's pregnant with our *second*. We aren't waiting like pretty boy CJ and Natasha over there."

Sashi laughed. "Are you always that mean about your brother?"

"Oh, you should see the two of them and Cole when they get going!" Sammi exclaimed. "They're like naughty boys in the schoolyard."

Sashi laughed again, and so did all three men in question. Natasha interjected, "You'll get used to it. Their warped humor tends to grow on you like the way the smell does after fishing trips."

A big bellowing laugh erupted and a huge man who looked like he must be the parent of the Powell boys came and gave Natasha a hug. "You're definitely a Powell now."

"No doubt about that." An older, dark-haired woman chimed in. "Hello, Sashi. We're Doug and Doris Powell. We love Cole and consider him our third son. We're so happy you're able to be out of the hospital, dear. I told Cole you could come and stay with us. But he's stubborn and insisted he was the only one who could take care of you." She paused, then added, "We're so sorry for your loss."

Tears smarted Sashi's eyes. None of these people knew her, but they came out to welcome her. It made her homesick for her parents. Yet it also made her yearn for this life with Cole. What would it be like to be pregnant with his baby and be part of this amazing loving community?

"Thank you, everyone, for coming here to welcome me. Especially those of you who don't know me. It has lifted my spirits more than you'll ever know."

"Oh, we're thrilled to meet you," Doris said warmly. "We've never had Cole call us up and invite us over to his house for a woman's sake. Believe me, it's *our* treat."

Sashi blushed before looking at Cole. She whispered her thanks.

"Just wait," he whispered back. "Mary has a surprise for you." He resumed his normal tone. "For now, are you hungry? Can I get you something to eat or drink?"

She nodded. "I'm starving for normal food. Can you get me anything that's not too much like the hospital's?"

Cole nodded and rose. Natasha came over and sat beside her. "Sashi, you look stunning in that dress."

"Well, you look stunning pregnant. Your husband helped saved my life. He's a hero."

Natasha gazed lovingly at CJ. "I have to agree. He'll always be my heroic fireman." Cole was back, and she got up to be with her husband.

Sashi watched as CJ rubbed Natasha's baby bump, then whispered something in her ear. The pair walked off then.

Cole put a tray of food in front of her. "Here are some treats. Chicken wings, pizza, chips and salsa, as well as chips and cheese dip. All recommended by the American Heart Association." His face was deadpan.

Sashi grinned. "This is definitely a treat. I haven't had this much food for so long I can't even remember."

"Dig in. I know I'm going to."

The party was great. Everyone ate and talked

and made sure they met Sashi and engaged her in conversation. Toward the end, Mary stood up and announced, "In Tlingit culture, we have a special welcome dance. My daughter, Abigail, myself and my father, Joe, will dance in celebration. We'll play our ceremonial drums and wear our robes known as Chilkat blankets. I hope you will enjoy this, Sashi."

The drums began, followed by the rhythmic chanting of the singers who swayed. Their regal dancing of such an ancient culture was beautiful for Sashi to behold. She watched their movements, so free and graceful, and was mesmerized by the intricate footwork and the to-and-fro movement of their hands.

Tears stung her eyes, she was so moved. When the dance was done, she clapped enthusiastically while the other onlookers cheered and whistled. She could see the pride in Joe, Mary and Abigail. They had a tradition of something beautiful and sacred.

She realized that she, too, had learned a tradition of dance passed down from the past. The tradition of ballet! It was something she could do—and pass on to future dancers.

She couldn't wait to heal completely and then strive for her dream: to teach children the art of ballet at her own studio. Her heart filled with gratitude to Mary who'd danced tonight to help Sashi remember who she was.

At last the party drew to a close. Sashi thanked people for their kindness in coming. Knowing she had no family or friends here, they'd come out on a dark foggy night to cheer her up and celebrate her discharge from the hospital. She would be forever grateful to them for that. Many of them promised to visit her soon. Cole saw everyone out as she rested on the couch, exhausted.

COLE WAS OUTSIDE WITH the departees. "Thanks for your help, guys." He knew Jake and CJ would be flying most of the guests home to Prince of Wales Island tonight. Everyone had really gone out of their way to help him.

"She's a wonderful girl, Cole," Doris said. "And a real beauty. How all you men manage to find such good-looking women is beyond me."

"She's just a friend," Cole insisted.

The forest service van erupted in laughter. Jake swatted him on the back. "When you're willing to talk reasonably, I'll be happy to give you some advice."

"I have no clue what you're talking about."

"I think he's the densest of the three of us, don't you think, Pops?" Jake looked at Doug.

"I don't know, Jakey. You were pretty stubborn with Sammi."

"We don't talk about that period," Jake muttered.

Sammi soothed her husband. "Dad? You know how sensitive he is about that time. He gets upset at the thought of my time away from him, so it's best not to bring it up."

"I was dense," Jake said, "but I knew I'd lost the girl I loved. Cole here won't even admit he has feelings for this woman." He faced Cole. "You're crazy about her! What is it with this doctor code of yours? She's not a patient anymore. What's holding you back?"

"She needs to get healthy and strong," Cole said. "I want her to return to the woman she was before. Once she's no longer afraid and has healed, then she can make good decisions."

Sammi eyed him solemnly. "Just make sure you don't play it too safe, Cole. You might push her out of your life. The chemistry between the two of you is obvious. That's a very special thing. Don't let her go."

"All right. Thank you, guys."

"Remember this," CJ said from the back of the van, "Sashi's never going to be the woman she was before. She'll be stronger and she's getting better. Make sure you're part of that process so she doesn't leave thinking she was just a duty to you. I've spent time with her. She's very smart. Give love a chance!"

Cole gave Jake a hug. "See ya soon, and thanks again."

"No problem, Dr. Love."

Cole stepped away from the laughter, then waved to them. The door closed and the van set off for the long journey home. He was a lucky man to have such good friends. They'd given him a lot to think about, but right now he needed to sleep on it.

He walked back into the house, grateful for the help with the cleanup. Everyone knew he wasn't the best housekeeper. His gaze flicked to the couch where he found Sashi fast asleep.

A new feeling of peace and contentment seized him knowing that the person he cared most about was in his home and soon would be settled for the night. He wanted to take her up to his bedroom in the loft, but that was definitely not going to happen. And he would definitely be taking a cold shower tonight.

Time to get her settled.

He went into the garage and grabbed her luggage. It took a little time to get her stuff put away. When he returned, he studied the woman sleeping so peacefully on the sofa. Her shimmering hair hung over the edge of the bolster.

Filled with emotion, he picked up this red-haired angel who'd come into his life and turned it upside down. What a blessing he'd had this apartment added on to the house for his parents when they came to visit. Jake mostly used this place when he couldn't get all the way home after a rescue. It had served many purposes, but none as important as this one.

The apartment had a kitchenette, dining room and a TV lounge area, all fashioned in the same style as the house. A hall led to the bedroom with a king-size bed. The intricately carved wood head and footboards were done in a light wood.

There was an en suite bathroom with a jetted tub and a walk-in shower done in travertine beige tiles. He was sure Sashi would like it. It should be easy for her to use and get around in.

Cole carried her into the bedroom and pulled the white sheets back before he set her down. He wasn't the doctor right now and didn't feel he had the right to undress her. He looked for her antibiotic and pain pill. She needed to take these so she could sleep.

Once he'd gone to the kitchenette for a glass of water, he returned and sat on the side of the bed, holding her up right in his arms. "It's time to take your medicine, Sashi. Can you put your pills in your mouth and swallow for me?"

He placed them in one hand and put the cup of water in the other. Obediently she put the pills in her mouth and swallowed. Then she lay back in his arms. He put the water on the dresser. Now it was time for him to leave, but all he could do was stare down at her perfect profile, wondering how to find the strength.

How many times had he imagined her in his bed? Her hair had splayed all over him and across the pillow. As he gently lowered her to a prone position, he studied her flawless skin and rosy lips. She didn't need any makeup. He'd never forgotten that night all those weeks ago up at Marshall's when they'd lost their inhibitions and kissed for hours.

The remembrance drove him to his feet. He'd best leave. He pulled up the comforter and tucked her in, and then with one last caress of her cheek, he left.

He headed straight up to his lair, as he liked to call it. His father, the architect, had enjoyed building this home. Cole loved all the light-colored materials his dad had used downstairs and he particularly liked the large windows. But he loved his bedroom with its Caribbean look. He even had a palm-style fan over his bed with posters of tropical places on his walls.

The downstairs might be a tribute to Native paintings and Wild West photos, but this was the real Cole up here. The tropics were what cheered him up. He'd never live anywhere but Alaska, but for vacation, he sure loved trips to the Caribbean and Hawaii.

He'd love to take Sashi with him, love to see her in a bikini, walk the beach at night with her. They'd lie in a hammock watching the stars at night while they talked about nothing, then make love until morning.

Cole removed his clothes, wondering how she was doing. But of course he *knew* how she was doing. She was fine!

He kicked his clothes away and headed for the bathroom and that cold shower.

SASHI WAS RUNNING FROM the bear. "No, no, no!" She could see Kendra running up the tree. "Please, Kendra, NO!"

She sat up, thrashing in the sheets of the darkened room, having no idea where she was. Panic seized her. "Help!" But her voice wouldn't work. She tried again. "Help!" Only a squeak came out. "Please." Her voice came out louder this time. "Help me!" There. Her voice was working again. "Please...somebody help me!"

Sashi looked around the room trying to find her crutches or walker. Where were they? Where was she? Where was Cole?

She got so scared she climbed onto the floor, careful not to bang her leg. Thank heaven her arms were strong. She crawled out of her room into the hall.

"Help, Cole! Where are you?" Tears streamed down her cheeks. He'd promised he wouldn't leave her. Where was he?

COLE HAD JUST WALKED OUT of the bathroom in pajama bottoms when he heard Sashi screaming for him. His first instinct was to grab the gun he kept by his bed at all times in case of an intruder, human or animal.

"I'm coming, Sashi!"

He raced down the stairs two at a time with his gun strapped across his back. He could hear her continued screaming. It terrified him. He couldn't comprehend what on earth could have happened in the past twenty minutes. When he turned the corner that led to the apartment, he flipped on the lights in the main room. Farther away he saw Sashi lying on the floor of the bedroom.

"Cole? Is that you?" she cried. "Where am I? What's going on? I'm so scared."

"It's me." He turned on the bedroom light.

Sashi looked wildly around the room. "I'm sorry. I had a nightmare. I get them every night. There's this bear coming for me. I've talked to Dr. Samuelson about it. He said he was going to prescribe medicine to help me not dream, but it doesn't work. Every time I close my eyes, I relive Kendra dying." Moisture bathed her face.

"Is that a gun?" she asked as he put it behind the door. He'd hoped she wouldn't see it.

"Yes." He crossed to her and picked her up. There was no way he could leave her in this kind of condition. She was terrified and needed comfort, and he was just the man to give it.

Chapter Seven

It was an amazing sensation to be pressed against Cole after her terror. Sashi had danced with many men before, but had never seen such a beautiful male body before. He had a rugged build with a smattering of blond hair across his pectorals. He had the physique of a man who lived outdoors, strong and lean.

She pulled herself together. "What were you doing with a gun?"

His gaze met hers. "We're in Alaska. When I heard you scream like that, I grabbed my gun to be ready for anything. I told you I'd protect you."

"So where are we going?"

"My room," Cole said calmly.

"Your what?" Sashi could barely believe her ears.

"My room. After this experience I'm not going to be able to sleep with you downstairs. With you having posttraumatic nightmares, you need to be watched. I'm going to take care of you."

"But in your bed?" Sashi's body filled with heat.

"If you're uncomfortable with that, I'll put my air mattress next to the bed. I know how bad those nightmares can be. I had them for years. I'm sorry. I should never have left you alone in a house you weren't familiar with. I blame myself."

"Please don't." She touched his cheek. "I should have told you about the nightmares."

He wanted her forgiveness. "No, I should've read your charts more thoroughly. It's my job as your doctor to make you comfortable while you stay here."

They reached his room, which was a complete contrast to the rest of the house. Cole placed her on top of the sea-green duvet. She took in the whole island theme and loved it. "This room is you, Cole!"

He smiled. "You think so?"

"I know. After listening to the music in the car and your carefree attitude, this room suits your personality completely. Who decorated the bottom floor of the house? It's beautiful, but more like a showplace."

"My dad, he's the architect," Cole replied. "My mom chose the furnishings. It looks like a miniature of their house. I drew the line at my bedroom."

"You must be proud of your dad to let him come in and build your home."

"Are you sure you didn't get your degree in psychology?"

Sashi laughed. "No, maybe then I wouldn't

be an in-debt dancer. I just figured that a child who would let his parents design and decorate his house must be proud of them. Or he wants their approval?"

"Maybe a little of both."

"And that's okay," she said.

"Do you want to change into one of my T-shirts to sleep?"

His question reminded her of the precarious arrangement, but she'd been in this outfit for most of the day, and something else to sleep in would be nice. She hated being a coward, but maybe having someone close by would help with the nightmares. Cole seemed pretty adamant about her sleeping with him.

"Sure. Could you help me to the bathroom since I don't have my crutches?"

Cole rummaged through his drawers for a shirt. She stared at his back, aching to really touch him. She'd touched some of him when they'd kissed back at Marshall's with their clothes on. Those kisses… when he was around she couldn't stop thinking of them.

In a minute he put on some music she hadn't heard before, a soothing jazz number. As she looked around his bathroom she saw various pictures of him with friends and two different beautiful women on the wall. He was a grown man. *Of course he's had girlfriends. Don't be silly.*

Focus. But as she did, she realized she'd only

been to the Caribbean once with Kendra and her family. The trip had been an absolute blast. Life with her best friend had always been a blast. She would always miss her...

"This is peaceful," Sashi said.

Cole nodded. "Do you dance to jazz?"

"I do, actually."

He grinned. "But I prefer music from abroad more. I love exotic vacations, and some *señoritas* taught me and my buddies some fun types of dancing."

Sashi took that as her cue to back down. Cole always played the friend card. "Well, the music's very soothing."

"I thought it might calm you down. I know music used to help me get my mind off my problems."

Of course. He was doing what a doctor would do. Find a treatment to calm the patient so she'd sleep.

"Thanks, Doc," she said. "Will you help me to the bathroom? Sorry to be such a pain." Sashi felt foolish sitting on his bed like a child. She wished she had her crutches. "Hey, Cole, you know? You've made me feel much better, so I think I'll be fine on my own back in my room."

COLE'S HEART LURCHED. There was no way he was going to let Sashi out of his sight tonight. He was still trying to recover from seeing her lying there on the floor terrified. Then to find out she was suffering badly from post-traumatic stress disorder. He wished Daniel had told him more. Had he known, he would've slept on the couch in her apartment.

What had upset her enough to want to go back downstairs? It was probably the talk about *señoritas*. He was such an ass. He'd been trying to show her that the *señoritas* meant nothing to him. Instead he'd made her think just the opposite and now she probably felt foolish.

"I can't let you leave, because I'm not comfortable with the idea. Come here. Let's get you ready." He could see the reticence in her eyes. "If you don't come over here, you can sleep in your dress. It's your choice."

She finally scooted over and let him pick her up. This time he couldn't help himself. He gathered her in his arms almost in time with the music. While one hand slid up her back possessively, she let him caress her leg like he'd wanted to do all night.

Her expression revealed she could tell the difference in his mood and her body melted into him. Her free hand moved up his bare arm with purpose, forming an arc until it found the spot on his neck to place for dancing. She ran her other hand up his chest and behind his neck. His body leaned into hers.

With little effort he picked her up, but this time he held her upright, wrapping his arms firmly around her. He let her left foot rest on his right foot as their bodies began to move to the music. Their eyes met and the attraction that had been between them at the beginning was still there. Sashi clung to Cole. Soon he was swaying her body to and fro so easily it felt as though they were one.

He couldn't believe how well the two of them fit. It was as if they were meant to be together. He held her close with one hand, then gently positioned her face so he could see those lips he'd been longing to kiss.

Cole rubbed his cheek against hers. Sashi let out a moan of pleasure and moved her lips closer to his. And then he kissed her.

SASHI OPENED HER MOUTH and deepened the kiss. This couldn't be happening. She was in heaven. She was dancing. Her body was moving and she was kissing the man of her dreams. It hit her then that she was in love with Cole. But did he love her? He constantly played this game of hot and cold with her. She didn't think she could handle it when he went back to being the caring doctor.

"We need to stop," she murmured, and pushed him away. "I don't know if you're simply feeling sorry for me right now, but I can't handle it. Will you take me to the bathroom and get me my crutches?" She was breathing fast, but her heart was pounding faster.

"I'm sorry, Sashi."

"Save it! Can you give me some privacy? I have pajamas in my suitcase. If you'll grab them for me, too. Do you have any idea how much I hate depending on you like this?" Anger had replaced her passion.

"I can only imagine. And for that, all I can say is how sorry I am." Cole carried her to the bathroom and put her down right next to the counter so she could have something to hold on to.

She was feeling too emotional. "I'd really like to go back to my room."

"I promise never to hurt you like that again. I'm worried about you being alone. PTSD is serious. Until we find the right meds to help you, night can be the worst of times. It doesn't matter where you sleep, I'll be in the room with you in my sleeping bag."

Sashi's face fell. "Fine. Will you just go?"

After he left, she splashed water on her face and used her finger as a toothbrush. She'd been insane to let Cole kiss her again. That and the dancing. It had felt good to move to music. She wasn't sure she'd be able to dance again. Everyone said she would, but what if she was broken forever?

She had to stop feeling sorry for herself. Mary had told her she'd be dancing one of these days. She was a wonderful physical therapist and Sashi trusted her. She had to fight her attraction to Cole and somehow come to understand that she wasn't responsible for Kendra's death.

Again the tears came. She rested her head on the counter. Kendra had been her best friend. This whole mess could have been prevented if Sashi had stopped her from going into the woods. How would she ever let go of the guilt?

Here she was stuck in Alaska with a man who at first had felt desire for her, but then had changed and felt only obligated to help her. Why he'd kissed her tonight made no sense. Like he'd said, he was sorry. She needed to remember that.

"I HAVE YOUR CLOTHES. Can I come in?" Cole asked.

She lifted her head. "Yeah. Just put them on the floor."

Cole felt like a heel. When he opened the door, he could see that Sashi had been crying. The woman had been through too much and the last thing she needed was to receive mixed signals from him. He put the clothes on the floor next to her. Understanding her need for independence, he propped her crutches against the counter.

While Sashi got dressed, Cole pulled out the sleeping bag he'd brought up. He rolled it out on an air mattress on the floor next to the bed, grabbed a pillow and lay down.

A few minutes later Sashi came out in a faded blue T-shirt and a pair of flannel pajama bottoms. He thought she looked sexier than ever. Obviously anything the woman wore turned him into a hormone-driven teenager. He watched as she climbed into his bed, trying not to imagine all kinds of things he shouldn't.

He reached for the glass of water and pills. "These are supposed to prevent the dreams. They helped me some nights when I was younger."

She looked at him and took a pill, gulping it down with the water he gave her. "Thanks. Have a good night's sleep, Cole."

"You, too." He climbed into his sleeping bag and for what seemed like hours listened to her breathe. At last he fell asleep.

Two weeks passed, and an exhausted Sashi entered the group therapy room using her walker. No one was here yet. She sat down and thought about her long day. She'd spent the morning working with Mary while they exercised her arms and good leg. Then she'd read until it was time for group therapy this afternoon.

Living with Cole was difficult. She found the daily routine tedious, as though they were going through the motions. There were looks of interest, moments their eyes found each other. Then they would slip back into the awkward friendship they'd created between them. Who gave a damn about the weather anymore? Sashi felt as if she was going to go crazy. Her attraction to Cole was growing stronger every day.

At some point she would need to fly to Prince of Wales Island and face Freddy. She was waiting for the DNA results to come back confirming that Freddy was indeed the father of Kendra's child. She'd told Trace about the pregnancy so the coroner would be cognizant of it before the autopsy.

Sashi was still mourning her friend and missing her family. Life was never going to be the same again—a difficult concept she had to come to terms with. In truth, Cole was just a person passing through her life, not really a part of it.

"Good afternoon." Dr. Samuelson walked in, dressed impeccably in a dark suit with a red tie.

"Hello, Doctor."

"How are you doing?" He took in her appearance. "You appear to be getting stronger."

"I am. Mary pushes me hard. And I push myself harder. Dancing is my life. I'm going to make my dream true."

She was still flushed and sweaty after working out. Luckily her leggings and T-shirt wore well. She'd pulled her hair into a tight bun.

"I can see that. There's new life in your cheeks and expression."

"I'm fighting a war with myself. I know I can win, but it's hard."

"In what way?"

"Panic attacks at anytime, terrible loneliness, nightmares, feelings of impending doom and depression, for starters." Sashi reached for a tissue.

The door opened and in walked Cole. He was in

scrubs and his white lab coat. Damn him. Nothing he wore made him unattractive.

"Glad you could join us, Cole."

"Sorry to be late, Daniel. There was a bad accident down the road. I had to prep a patient for the O.R." Sashi noticed the dark smudges beneath his eyes. He hadn't been sleeping and she wondered why.

"In emergencies we can postpone your therapy," the doctor assured him.

"I know, but today is special. Sashi is finally ready to tell her story. I didn't want her to have to wait any longer than necessary."

"You look tired. Are you sure you don't need a break from things?"

"Can we talk about me later?" Cole shot him a look that said he was done talking.

The tension in the room made Sashi feel claustrophobic, like being trapped inside a blanket.

"I don't think I can talk about anything with all my bad feelings." She buried her face in her hands. "I just don't want to talk."

"Okay. Let's try something else." She could hear Dr. Samuelson moving chairs around. When she looked up, she saw two chairs facing each other.

"What are you doing?"

"I want you to take a seat in one of the chairs."

Self-consciously Sashi got up and, leaning on the walker, moved to the chair closest to herself. She sat. "What do I do now?"

"I want you to look at that empty chair and pretend Kendra's sitting there. I want you to tell her how you feel. Then I want you to go to the other chair and respond as if you were Kendra. Okay?"

Horrified, Sashi looked at Cole and then at the doctor. "This is even worse."

"Go on, Sashi," the doctor pushed. "Tell Kendra how you feel. I think it will make you feel better." Cole nodded in agreement.

She shuddered and took a deep breath. "Kendra? I'm sorry." A sob came out. Sashi grabbed her tissue and dabbed her eyes. "I'm so sorry I didn't stop you from walking out the door of the cabin. I blame myself for you leaving. I had no idea you were pregnant. I should have known or figured it out.

"I don't know how, but I should have come up with some way to stall you or talk reason into you. I should have kept you from leaving the cabin after you and Freddy fought. Instead I just blindly followed you out that door.

"Why I didn't use the receiver Joe gave me sooner, I don't know. I was delirious with pain. But I regret every moment of every day since you've been gone that *you're* gone and *I'm* here. It's not fair. You've always been the most unselfish, kind person I've ever known. Plus...you were pregnant." Sashi completely broke down.

"Now, Sashi," Dr. Samuelson said, "I want you to switch places. I want you to be Kendra and answer Sashi. Do you think she would be angry you lived instead of her? Do you think she would want you to walk around with all those feelings?"

Sashi looked at Dr. Samuelson, then Cole. "This is going to be so hard."

"Therapy is never easy, Sashi. But in time I promise it will get easier. So, go to the other chair."

Sashi was angry. She grabbed her walker and placed it in front of her. If that ass wanted her to do it, then she would. She put her hands on both handles and began to lift herself up, but she found herself physically drained after sharing her feelings with "Kendra." She fell back in the chair. "Damn."

"Let me help her," Cole said.

"No. She has to do this alone."

Sashi reached deep within and summoned the energy. She grabbed onto those handles and lifted herself. Then she worked across the small space to the other chair. Such a space shouldn't seem like such a far distance, but today it felt like an eighteen-hour practice session. She collapsed into the second chair.

She was panting but felt proud of herself for crossing the gap to Kendra. For that was exactly what it had been. A mental gap in her mind she hadn't wanted to breach. But the doctor had made her do it.

"All right, Sashi. What would Kendra say to you?"

Sashi looked at the empty chair and saw an empty person. Her voice wobbled when she spoke.

"Sashi, babe...what's happened to you, sweetie? Where is my friend? I...I don't see her anywhere. I heard what you said, but you know it's all crap, right? I've always been taller and stronger than you. When have you ever stopped me from doing anything?

"Why would you blame yourself for what happened? I don't blame you. I wouldn't blame you for anything. I love you, babe. Always have, always will." Sashi's body began to shake as tears poured from her eyes.

"Sweetie, I'm glad you lived," Kendra/Sashi went on. "You get a second chance at life. Live it. Go after your dreams. You've always dreamed bigger than anyone I've ever known and I've always been proud of you." Sashi wiped away tears and looked at Dr. Samuelson, then at Cole, whose eyes were full of tears.

"Did you hear yourself, Sashi?" Dr. Samuelson asked her. "Did you hear your friend Kendra give you permission to forgive yourself?"

"Yes, I heard her. I know she would want me to move on, but it's hard. I miss her so much. I feel like part of my heart has been ripped out. She was like a sister to me."

"You'll always miss her, and it's okay to feel sad. But it's not okay to feel guilty for her death. The same goes for you, Cole. This is a mantra I want both of you to take with you today. It's okay to miss them, but not to feel guilty that they're gone."

"Okay," Sashi whispered.

Cole looked at the doctor. "Does this mean I quote it to myself daily?" he asked.

"You quote it whenever you feel guilty about losing Luke. Today went very well, Sashi. Let's look at a meeting next Wednesday. Does that work?"

"Yes," she said. "My day's are pretty well planned out."

"That should be fine," Cole said. "I'll clear it with the E.R. desk. Thanks, Daniel."

SASHI THUMPED INTO PHYSICAL therapy and checked in at the desk. "Hi, Debra, how are you today?"

"Good," Debra replied. "Sashi, you're handling those crutches really well. Take a seat and Mary will be right with you."

Sashi gazed into the room she'd come to think of as a studio until she could begin dancing again. A lot of stationary bikes. Minitrampolines, bars and beds for patients to lie on were among the other kinds of equipment.

She saw Mary walking toward her. She thought, not for the first time, how beautiful Mary was with coffee-colored skin and long hair plaited tightly, showing off the lovely angles of her face.

"My favorite patient!" Mary declared. "My father is jealous of the time I spend with you. Good chance he'll show up here sometime."

Sashi smiled. She'd enjoyed many meals with Joe, Mary, Eric and Abigail—the very nature of

Cole's job kept him at work late or overnight and he wasn't around for supper. At times Sashi feared she was an imposition to Joe's family, but then she could see it hurt them when she turned them down. "Tell Joe he can come anytime."

Mary smiled, then sobered. "Today, Sashi, we're going to work on your balance. I want you to stand on this low trampoline and bounce this ball back and forth against the wall." She handed Sashi the ball.

Sashi looked at the trampoline and vowed she would master the task. Half an hour later Sashi was performing the assignment well, if not with the perfection she wanted. She knew that to others, her recovery was going very well. But she was a ballerina. Would she ever regain all her balance?

She took her frustration out on the ball, imagining every time she threw it at the wall that it was Freddy's head. Once she was strong enough to go home, she was going to give him a piece of her mind. She realized there was no legal action she could take, but she had to face the coward. He had to be made to know that he was a big part of the reason Kendra died, and so horribly.

"Sashi, you amaze me," Mary said at last. "Your drive and persistence are going to have you dancing before you know it. Let's go and get you on the stationary bike for a while."

With a new ease, Sashi grabbed her crutches and headed to the bike. It made her miss traditional road biking, but she tried to count it as a great blessing that she was moving at all. On the stationary bike, she pedaled away the pain, frustration and confusion over what to think about Cole. What *was* going on between them?

COLE ARRIVED EARLY AT the group therapy session. There were a few things he needed to go over before Sashi came in. He'd taken a quick shower, pulled on some jeans and a button-down shirt. It had been over twenty-fours since he'd seen Sashi and he wanted to look his best.

Daniel leaned back in his chair. "What did you want to talk to me about, Cole?"

Cole came right out with it. "I'm falling in love with Sashi. I know she's healing emotionally, and physically, but when do you think I can finally tell her how I feel? Or will it ruin the healing experience? Daniel, I'm losing sleep. For the first time in my life I'm at a loss over a woman."

"Have you talked with Sashi and explored how she feels about you? This could be one-sided. It's up to you to find out how she's feeling after all this turmoil. This place—" he gestured at the room— "is a great forum to do it. Of course you can also do it privately."

Cole looked up at the ceiling, then breathed deeply. "I should've known I'd get no answers from you."

"This is your life, Cole. I'm not here to tell you how to live it."

"All right. I'll talk to her tonight."

As SASHI OPENED THE DOOR to the room for group therapy, she hoped Cole would be present. He'd been busy and had missed a few sessions. Therapy was always better when he was there, of course. Her feelings were mixed, but having the connection to another person who'd been through a similar trauma was important.

When she walked in, she smelled the tangy aftershave Cole wore, and her body relaxed immediately. Cole looked up and gave her a smile that melted problems away, at least for the moment. He had a remarkable ability to lift her spirits and make her heart flutter at the same time.

Sashi took her seat next to Cole, then looked to Dr. Samuelson for the session to start. Then she remembered that one of them—Cole or her—had to start talking. That was the rule. Might as well be her.

"I'm ready to tell my story today," she said. And she did. The recounting of her harrowing story brought out a lot of pain, anger and sadness.

"Dr. Samuelson?" she said when she was done. "Will you pull up the picture I sent you via email last night?"

On the doctor's screen were two girls in waders: a tall brunette and a short redhead. It was the last day Kendra was alive. "I love this picture," Sashi said. "It was taken right after we landed at Red Bay. Kendra was having the giggles since the waders came up to my chin. We both knew I looked ridiculous and it was—" Sashi's eyes began to fill "—the last time I heard her laugh."

"How do you feel now, Sashi? Now that you've shared your story with us."

She thought for a moment. "I feel anger and extreme guilt."

"Why guilt? You didn't make your friend run into the forest. Let me put it this way. Has either one of you seen the movie *Speed*?"

The two answered yes.

"There's a great scene in the movie that discusses survivors guilt. Start thinking about when the woman on the bus is blown up by the villain of the show. Sandra Bullock feels guilty because she's driving the bus. It takes Keanu Reeves's character to explain to her that it's okay not to feel guilty that it wasn't her.

"I want both of you to realize there is no fairness in the world. You can choose to feel guilty, but what's the point? You'll either be a victim or you'll suffer from guilt. You eventually have to learn to accept that some people do well in life and some don't. It's just the luck of the draw. No reason for them to deserve it."

"That's a lot to think about, Dr. Samuelson,"

Sashi said. "I think I'm going to watch that movie on my computer tonight."

"Why don't you let me watch it with you?" Cole gave her a smile that made her shiver.

"Sounds like a plan."

"I'll see you two soon," said the doctor.

COLE PULLED THE RANGE ROVER into the hospital's pickup bay. In a long-sleeve black tunic top with gray leggings, her hair swaying in the wind, Sashi looked stunning as she waited for him. He jumped out of the car to help her climb inside.

"Would you like to eat out tonight? I haven't been able to show you around Ketchikan the way I would have liked. Are you up for going to dinner?"

He knew on the outside he seemed cool, but deep down he was nervous. What was she going to say? He'd never been nervous with a woman before, yet now he was worried about how she'd respond. It shouldn't bother him so much when ultimately she would go back to Virginia and open a dance studio.

Sashi had a dreamy look on her face as she answered. "I'd love to."

UPON RETURNING TO HIS HOUSE, Sashi hurried to her room where she pulled out a new outfit she and Mary had picked up in town. She'd purchased it with the cash she'd saved for the trip with Kendra and the flight home. Tonight Sashi was thrilled she'd bought the blouse and skirt, even if the purchase was a little extravagant. The white silky blouse tied around her waist, and the red skirt hugged her hips, then flared at her knees.

After completing her makeup and curling her hair, Sashi felt like her old self. She exited the little apartment and was met at the door by Cole, who looked quite dashing in dark jeans and light gray sweater.

As Cole's eyes slowly took in every inch of her, she found herself breathless.

His voice was deep when he spoke, almost like a caress. "You look way too beautiful for a night out in Ketchikan. I wish I was taking you to some ritzy restaurant in a big city, and then to the ballet or symphony."

"I would say the same thing about you. Except you have this way of looking comfortable in any situation. One of the many traits I find fascinating about you."

Cole flashed her a crooked smile before taking her by the arm to help her out to the car.

They pulled up to a restaurant near the ocean called Luigi's. An Italian restaurant was the last place she'd thought he'd take her. "I didn't know they had a restaurant like this in Ketchikan."

"It's the only one. I was hardly going to take you to a bar and buy you a beer." Cole reached over and fingered a lock of her hair. "I know you're from the

East Coast. They have a different mentality than we do up here in Alaska."

Sashi turned and faced him. Their eyes locked and she was completely caught up in his gaze. "I'm learning to love a lot of things about Alaska. I like the casualness and the easygoing natures of the people I've met."

"I'm glad. It's good to know you don't hate Alaska after your experience."

Sashi took his comment in to think about later as the valet opened her door. In a flash Cole was at her side and soon the aroma of Italian food filled her nostrils. The layout and design of the restaurant—stone floors and stucco walls decorated with fake flowers—screamed Italian, and she was utterly charmed.

A dark-haired man of medium height swept into the room. "*Dottore.* Welcome to my *ristorante.*"

"It's good to see you, Luigi. How are you doing? How's your family?"

"*Bene, bene.* Life is good to me. Ah, I see you've brought a *bellissima* woman to my place. I will prepare special meal for both of you. No charge."

Sashi looked at the owner and could see the great affection he had for Cole. "Luigi, do tell me how you two know each other."

"For you, *bella,* anything! Dr. Cole delivered our last baby in his car in the middle of a snowstorm. It was December."

Sashi's heart brimmed over with feelings for

Cole. Dinner out at this restaurant and now this story…it seemed Cole was the town hero. Certainly he was *her* hero. "I believe it. Cole saved me, too. He's quite the miracle worker."

Luigi nodded. "I go now to make your meal. I'll have my hostess seat you at our best table."

Her thank-you and Cole's came out at the same time.

Soon they were ushered to a secluded table, lit by candlelight and overlooking the water. Cole seated Sashi, then sat across from her.

Over the next hour, as they sipped an excellent red wine, Luigi delivered course after delicious course. At last Sashi sat back in her chair, replete.

"I love the cooking of southern Italy, all the seafood," she said. "I was a fool to think at first it wouldn't work up here, but of course it would. There's no better fish than up here in Alaska. Thank you for this delicious meal."

Cole had ordered cappuccinos for them both, and after a sip, he said, "Sashi, I have something I need to ask you."

"What?" She felt so relaxed and happy in this serene environment. In that moment she realized she wanted a life with Cole in Alaska. She could open her dance studio here and they could be together. At this point in their relationship that could be wishful thinking. She had issues to deal with— the guilt about Kendra and her anger at Freddy. And those needed to be taken care of first, didn't they? Not to mention going home to Virginia and facing the Knights. She had to ask them to forgive her for not taking better care of Kendra. She also needed to thank them for paying her medical costs. She never could have afforded the care herself. Her brow furrowed in consternation.

COLE HAD BEEN ABOUT TO SAY what he wanted to say so desperately from his heart. But as he looked at Sashi, he could tell she was tired and had something else on her mind. He would talk to her later tonight.

"Are you up for watching the movie Dr. Samuelson recommended tonight?"

Her eyes shone with happiness at that suggestion. "Yeah, let's get out of here. I feel stuffed." Sashi patted her flat stomach. Those green eyes flashed back at his. "The food was delicious and the company was wonderful."

Cole's body raged with desire for her. Didn't she know how her words toyed with his emotions? The last thing he wanted to do was go home and watch a movie. But he knew how fragile everything was. He needed to play his hand carefully so as not to scare her away.

"All right, let's get going."

SASHI HAD TO BEAT COLE to the couch in the TV room. She snuggled into one corner so Cole wouldn't feel obliged to sit beside her. It was a self-protective measure, for there'd been other nights when he'd chosen to sit in the middle of the sofa.

Sashi heard a door close and watched Cole come down the stairs in sweats and T-shirt. His biceps bulged out the sleeves and his brawny shoulders were to die for. As he came closer, she noticed his unshaven face and slightly mussed hair. All she could think about now was kissing the man senseless.

She watched him quickly load the movie, then was surprised when he asked out right, "Mind if I sit close to you tonight?" With that he sat down right next to her. He reached over the leather couch and grabbed another throw blanket.

Sashi was a person who liked being busy. But since the encounter with the bear, it was unbelievable how much TV and how many movies she'd watched. She also couldn't believe how hard it was to sit so close to the man she was in love with and do nothing about it. Inside she felt warm, as if heated honey was running through her veins. She was aware of every movement and gesture he made.

Right before the scene they'd discussed in therapy came on, Cole reached over and pulled her tight into the warmth of his embrace. The intoxicating scent of cologne, the feel of his arm around her body, the occasional caress of her neck…if she thought she was warm before, she was a five-alarm fire now!

The sensual feelings caused her to breathe a sigh and press her body into his touch. Suddenly the TV was off and Cole's lips were on her neck. She shivered and angled back for him to kiss her more. The touch of his lips on her throat, her jaw, began to drive her wild.

Cole adjusted her body and gently laid her down beneath him. Sashi looked into those golden eyes and believed she'd found paradise. The raw desire he apparently felt for her was her complete undoing. Her hands reached up to grasp his jaw and bring his lips down on hers. There was an ache only he could satisfy and she knew it.

"Sashi…" Cole spoke with a husky voice. His mouth was just a few inches from her face. "I wanted to talk to you tonight but—"

One of Sashi's fingers moved to seal his lips. "Shh. Right now I don't want to talk." She drew his face down and began to kiss his jaw. She loved the feel of the bristles. Here was a real man, a man she could trust and depend on. Her hero.

She could tell Cole was done with her light play. He tipped her head up with one of his hands and brought his mouth to hers. Sashi felt an explosion of heat and lost all thought except to deepen the kiss. Their tongues met and danced.

Cole pulled her closer and closer until they were one. He rubbed her back, then put his hand underneath her shirt. It was only when he was about to touch her breasts she pulled away.

COLE FELT SASHI STOP. In seconds he was up and off her. *What in hell just happened?* Out of the corner of his eye he saw her sit up and turn to face him in an old T-shirt and hospital scrubs for pants.

"Sashi, what is it? Did I do something wrong? Did I hurt you?" Cole was fighting to get his emotions under control. This is why he'd stayed away. He knew Sashi had problems. He'd been a fool to make a move on her tonight. Why hadn't he listened to Daniel and talked to her first?

The longer he looked at her, the more pensive her face grew. When she was finally ready to talk, her eyes were sad. Cole cursed himself. Why hadn't he just let things continue the way they were— hands off.

"I'm sorry, Cole. It's not you. I haven't been intimate with a man in a long time. My mind started racing with stuff like, how will this affect our living together? I'm sorry. I still have so much to do before I leave Alaska. And then there's the problem of how I'll handle leaving you...."

Cole sat back and folded his arms. Of course she would have these concerns. So did he. So why did he make that mistake and push the limit when he had no idea yet what would come of their relationship? But what were the other things she had to do before she left Alaska?

"I'm the one who's sorry," he said. "I want to help you with all the things you need to do before you leave Alaska."

"I shouldn't impose on you any more."

He shook his head. "Sashi, from the moment we met there's been an incredible chemistry between us. I've never felt anything like it before. I know you live on the other side of the country and have another life planned out, but until you leave, I want you to know I'll help in whatever way I can."

Tears filled Sashi's eyes. "You've done everything for me. I owe you so much and I can't thank you enough. Right now I don't know about my future. There are things I need to take care of."

"Listen to me," he said. "Don't you realize that by helping you, it helps me to heal, too?" Cole searched her eyes for understanding. He could tell she was giving in when she leaned back against the sofa.

"I need to continue to learn to forgive myself for what happened to Kendra," she responded. "I don't know if I will ever be able to have a healthy relationship with a man if I don't. I have anger toward Freddy and have to face him, Cole. I've made some inquiries, but apparently no one has seen him lately at Marshall's."

"I know the law can't hurt him," Cole said, "but the Knights called yesterday with the DNA results on the baby's father. It's Freddy. Thank heaven Trace listened to you and took a sample when they were investigating the bear attack. Freddy had such a hangover at the cabin, I don't think he knew what he was saying yes to." Cole paused and looked at her. "Now, is there anything else?"

She nodded. "I need to find a way to say thank you to the Knights. I hope one day they will forgive me, too."

"I'll help you as much as I can with finding Freddy and a way to thank the Knights, but the Knights don't have anything to forgive you *for*. They don't hold you responsible. They've heard how you threw yourself in front of the bear to protect Kendra. This is something you need to discuss with Dr. Samuelson."

"Fair enough," she murmured. "Cole?" There was panic in her voice.

"Yes?"

"How did you face going back into the wilderness again? I love the outdoors and I know I need to conquer my fear, but how am I going to do it?"

"That's one problem I can help you with. In our next group therapy session I'll tell you and Daniel my idea."

A faint smile crossed her lips. "Thanks for being so understanding tonight. I feel lucky to have you in my life."

Her compliment was proof that the connection they had was real and special. He just needed to give her that time to heal. And he knew exactly how he was going to help her.

Chapter Eight

It had been a week since that night on Cole's couch. They had gone back to being friends, if you could call it that, Sashi thought. She wished she had more answers. Her heart was ready to marry, to open her studio and to have kids. Unfortunately the timing was off. She had to fix herself before she could get involved. But the idea of distancing herself from Cole was killing her. She was walking a slippery slope.

Today after group therapy Sashi was going to see the orthopedic surgeon. Hopefully her cast could come off today. It dawned on her that she'd been living with Cole for over two months. If she was doing as well as the doctor thought, then she'd be able to fly home in a week or two. But the mere thought of leaving Cole made her feel sick.

The kitchenette door opened and Dr. Samuelson walked in with a steaming cup of coffee.

"Do you ever miss New York?" Sashi asked.

He gave her a big smile and nodded. "Yes, that's why I fly there as often as I can."

"There is something wonderful about the big city, isn't there? But I'm also learning to love Ketchikan and the beauty of nature out here."

"They're definitely two different worlds. So tell me what's going on with you. Cole will be here as soon as he can."

The door flew open and a flustered Cole in scrubs walked in.

"It's good to see you, Cole. We were just about to start," Dr. Samuelson said in his deep, steady voice. Go ahead, Sashi."

"Well…I wanted to discuss my anger. I have a lot of anger built up. I'm finding myself consumed with rage against Freddy Marshall. The Knights have proof that he's the father. I feel the need to confront him. Tell him how I feel. That if he hadn't denied that the child was theirs, Kendra wouldn't have run out into the night. I would have been able to stop her before she went too far and we would never be in this situation."

The doctor cocked his head. "I want to tell you two stories of different Holocaust survivors. One is the story of a man called Primo Levi. He survived Auschwitz. Yet the rest of his life he was a ghost of a man, letting the memory of the concentration camps control him. He may have lived a long life, but his death was thought to be a suicide. It's been said that Primo died in Auschwitz.

"The other story is about a seventeen-year-old woman named Judith Strick. Once she was freed from Auschwitz, she joined the Russian army, but then requested to move to Israel and there she married and became a housewife. She'd purged herself of all the anger and guilt. Judith was ready to move on.

"I think it's very important for both of you to face any anger you feel and combat it in a way that will make you feel better."

"That's what I want to do!" Sashi exclaimed. "After learning what can happen to people if they carry this guilt and anger around and do nothing about it, I know I need to find Freddy."

Cole spoke up. "I can see I need to do some work on my own, too. I've believed that my parents have always been angry at me for what happened. I've feared they thought I could have done more. I need to talk with them and see if this is true. I've isolated myself for the past twenty years now. It's time to move forward."

Dr. Samuelson wrote everything down as fast as possible on his yellow pad of paper. When he glanced up, Cole said to him, "How else can Sashi and I let go of this guilt?"

The doctor nodded. "All right. I'd like both of you to write letters to the loved ones you've lost. When you're ready, I want you to share them with someone in a meaningful place. Let yourself be forgiven. Remember their deaths were the result of circumstances, *not* your wrongdoing."

"Okay," Sashi said, "but just one more thing. How do I face going back out into the great outdoors?"

Dr. Samuelson sat forward in his chair and eyed her frankly. "You just go out there and face your fears. It's just like riding a bike. You're surrounded by people who care and know the area well. I'm sure you can find someone to take you into the wilderness."

"I'll be happy to take you," Cole said. "I know a beautiful place this time of year."

"It's settled, then. I'll see you back next Tuesday. Have a great weekend and good luck with your homework."

WHILE COLE RETURNED TO the E.R., Sashi headed to the orthopedic doctor's office. When she used her crutches to step into the examining room, an older man who looked like a mountaineer walked in. Sashi's adrenaline surged. Here was the man who would tell her if she could have her cast removed. She hoped this part of the healing process was over.

"Hello, Sashi," Dr. Meers said. "Let's get some final X-rays. I think we'll be taking that cast off today."

"That's wonderful! Finally some good news!"

"Remember, your leg will be a bit atrophied.

But with continued therapy, you'll be dancing in no time."

The rest of the afternoon passed quickly with further X-rays to make sure the bone had healed correctly. The cast came off and as he'd said, her leg and foot looked shriveled and weak. But no matter. She knew how to train. She'd come this far and she would heal. As for the inside of her, only time would tell.

Cole was stuck in the E.R., so Sashi tagged along with Mary. She loved going with Mary to pick up Abigail from school. That little girl had a million dance questions and Sashi wished she could show her all the moves. One day she hoped to send Abigail a DVD answering those questions. Her time with the little girl crystallized her desire to pursue her dream and open her dance studio for children.

"ARE YOU EXCITED?" COLE flashed Sashi a brilliant smile as he piloted his Cessna toward Humpback Lake in the Misty Fjords National Monument.

Excited was only part of what Sashi was feeling. She was also very grateful to him for helping her face her fears out in the bush.

It was such a new feeling to be taken care of so completely. She wondered what he had planned. Before they'd boarded the plane, she saw he'd loaded the rear with some items.

In khakis and a blue fleece pullover, he looked

as though he could be a male model on a cover for a outerwear magazine. He was always full of surprises. Watching him made her heart skip all over the place. She had no idea how she'd leave him once she'd healed physically and mentally. That was something she would have to face when the time came.

Needing to redirect her thoughts, she looked out the window. The sight took her breath away. They were flying over a sea of mountain peaks covered in pine trees. No wonder people loved the country up here. She'd forgotten how green the Tongass rain forest was.

Just over the horizon she saw a sea-green body of water shining in the sun. As the Cessna drew closer, it began its descent to the lake, which sat in the valley between enormous forested peaks that rose thousands of feet into the sky.

Cole made a perfect landing, taxiing to a cabin tucked up against a peak hidden away from the world. The two-story cabin with a porch had a beautiful waterfall only twenty feet behind it. This had to be one of the most beautiful places on earth. Ferns and lichen surrounded the cabin, creating a lush atmosphere that was romantic beyond belief. Too romantic for the man who'd been treating her as a friend, she thought, but definitely a good choice for helping her to not be afraid of going into the backcountry.

The plane pulled up to the dock. Cole killed the

power, then jumped out and tied everything up. "You stay put," he said. "I'm going to go check the cabin out to make sure it's safe. I'll be right back." He grabbed a couple of bags and his gun from the rear of the plane. "Shouldn't be longer than five minutes."

"Sounds good to me." Sashi watched as the man she loved trekked to the cabin and disappeared inside. She bit her lip and thought how safe she felt out here with Cole. He was an amazing man. Again she wondered how she would ever be able to walk away from him and the wonderful life here.

COLE ENTERED THE CABIN he and Jake had used a few times when they'd been fishing. He'd always thought it was the kind of getaway a woman would appreciate. Heading to the stove, he got the fire going to make the place toasty.

What would Sashi think? Would she like this place? He hoped it would help allay some of her fears.

She was a sophisticated woman, used to big cities like New York and the warmer climes of Virginia. Would she ever really be happy here? Or would he be willing to leave all this and go southeast to start a new life with her? He knew he was thinking too far ahead. For now they both had to heal. Hopefully they'd do it together.

He put the picnic basket full of goodies on the table. Time to go get her. When he walked outside, he was hit by the beauty of the state he lived in. He loved Alaska. This land of mountains and sea was in his blood. It brought joy to his heart and made his spirits soar.

Smiling, he approached the plane. In the passenger seat sat the woman he loved. A beautiful woman inside and out. Today she wore a white fleece jacket and form-fitting jeans with her feet tucked into boots. She'd done her hair in some sort of thick braid with free pieces hanging over her shoulder.

"You look sensational today," he said when he reached her.

Her head went back and she looked at him as if he was crazy. "Thanks," she said with a small smile.

"Let's get you out of here and into the cabin. Then you can move around on crutches."

Sashi bit her lip. "Can I ask you a favor?"

Cole's brows lifted in curiosity. "Sure."

"Could you take me to that waterfall?" She pointed. "It looks unreal."

It took some time, but Sashi managed to get to the waterfall with the help of her crutches and Cole's strong arm.

She found herself a bit bewildered by the change in Cole out here in the woods. He appeared so relaxed, he melded with the landscape. "I can tell you love it out here," she said.

Cole nodded. "You're absolutely right. There's nothing in the world like the rain forest up here."

"Thank you for bringing me and sharing this beautiful place. I haven't felt nervous at all."

He brought his hand up to touch her cheek. "I'm glad."

IF LIFE HAD BEEN DIFFERENT and the bear attack hadn't happened, would she and Cole have found their way to each other? Quite possibly. After all, they'd had a connection before the accident. But the attack had made their relationship take a turn she didn't fully understand.

She decided to focus on the sheer beauty of this place, as they wended their way through the ferns and pines. It was almost unreal. The cascading waterfall might have come right out of a fairy tale.

"It's pure magic out here," she said.

"I couldn't agree more," he said.

Their eyes met. His seemed to darken. "The day isn't over yet." With those words he gave her a quick kiss on her lips. The sensation on her mouth made her warm all over, causing her to lose concentration. Then some raindrops struck her face. "How could it be raining?" she cried in surprise. She looked up at the sky, amazed that a storm had rolled in so quickly.

"I was hoping it might do that." Cole looked excited. "Let's get inside before it starts to pour."

He scooped her up, crutches and all, and made a

beeline for the cabin. Just as they entered, the heavens let loose and the rain came down fiercely, pelting the roof and the windows. Cole put her down at the picnic-style table. Sashi was grateful he'd already started a fire. The warmth from the stove had already put out heat and the cabin felt cozy.

She looked at him. "Just out of curiosity," she asked, "why were you hoping it would rain?"

"I'll show you in a little while. For now you need to trust me."

Sashi trusted him completely. Still, she wondered what he was up to. It wasn't like him to be coy.

COLE HAD REACHED AN IMPASSE. How was he going to tell her that he'd distanced himself from her because he didn't want to take advantage of her when she was vulnerable? For the first time in his life he needed to let his guard down with a woman, put his heart on the line and tell her that he loved her. What else could he do?

"Are you hungry?" he asked. "I've packed us a delicious meal."

Sashi laughed. "You made us a meal?"

That laugh was music to his soul. It showed how relaxed she was here, how happy she was. He traced an index finger down her cheek. "No. I had it delivered to the plane from a delicatessen in town. They import excellent food."

The look of shock on Sashi's face was priceless. "Why would you do this for me?"

"Because you're special and I wanted this day to be unforgettable."

Her green eyes turned translucent as they misted over. Cole could tell she was touched. He opened the basket and pulled out a checkered red-and-white tablecloth, which he spread out over the table.

Then he began to pull out the other items in the basket: a fresh baguette, a variety of cheeses, fresh fruit, a decadent chocolate torte, plates, utensils, champagne and flutes to drink from.

"COLE, THIS IS WONDERFUL!"

"I hoped it would be. So how are you feeling now? Nervous?"

"No. Very content."

When she looked out the window, she saw the reason Cole had hoped for rain. There were waterfalls cascading down the mountain in every direction she looked, fed by the downpour. And now that the fast-moving storm was passing and the sun was peeking out, multiple rainbows had formed over the falls. She turned to Cole.

"So this is why you wanted rain," she whispered in awe. "You wanted me to see this. If there's a heaven, I imagine this is what it looks like."

Cole grasped her hand and helped her to the door, then swung it wide so they could see the stunning views in the open. "It *is* heaven here," he said.

"I brought you so you could see that nature doesn't have to be scary. It can be beautiful."

So beautiful it took her breath away. She watched the last of the waterfalls cascade over the ledges. She looked up to thank Cole, but stayed silent at the desire she saw blazing in his golden eyes.

"Sashi," he said, "when we met up at Marshall's, that was one of the most special nights of my life."

"For me, too," she breathed.

"When I found out you were hurt, I—"

His cell rang, cutting off what he was going to say. "It's my two-way emergency phone. I have to take it. One moment and we'll talk some more." Cole kissed her forehead, then headed farther outside, while she maneuvered herself back to the table.

He'd looked put out that they'd been interrupted, she thought, but she was just as disappointed. Sashi was dying to know what he'd been about to tell her. She prayed the call was nothing too serious.

As COLE ANSWERED, HE WAS READY to kill whoever was on the other end of the phone. "Cole Stevens here.

"Cole, it's Trace."

"Trace, there'd better be a damn good reason you're calling me."

"There is. Jake thinks he's found Freddy for you."

That was a different matter. "When and where do I meet you for rendezvous?"

"We're at the Powells' right now. Get here as soon as you can."

THE FLIGHT TO CRAIG felt ominous. Sashi's insides were twisted with tension. The beautiful green mountains they'd passed as they'd flown in to Humpback Lake now had a dusting of snow on the peaks. It changed the view dramatically, just like the feeling inside her. Cold.

With Freddy at last in their sights and her need to confront him close to being fulfilled, she feared she would lose Cole forever. She needed to begin to separate herself from him because her time in Alaska was coming to a close.

Now that she was more mobile, she needed to take control of her life. She wasn't sure what that entailed yet, but she couldn't handle this back-and-forth thing with Cole any longer. As soon as she faced Freddy, she planned on heading home without Cole's knowledge. Her heart already ached at the thought of what she knew she needed to do.

They made a quick pit stop in Ketchikan to refuel and to grab some clothes for a couple of days until Freddy was apprehended.

She felt so grateful to Cole and all his friends for helping her find the coward who had gone into hiding. This would allow her to share her feelings.

Who knew if it would help? But at this point she was desperate to try.

Today's experiment of going into the wilderness seemed to have worked to reduce her fear of the outdoors. Next she'd have to try going into the Blue Ridge Mountains back home. She wouldn't have Cole to lean on, but she'd have her mom and dad.

Once they were back on the plane headed to Prince of Wales Island, she had mixed feelings. This is where her nightmare had begun, yet as Dr. Samuelson had told her, she couldn't always think of the island that way. She had to be strong and face her fears. It was important to remember the wonderful memories here, too. The good ones with Kendra and the first time she'd met Cole. Those were the ones she would hold on to for a lifetime.

"Sashi? You've barely said a word since we left the cabin." Cole glanced over at her. "Do you want to talk about what you're feeling?"

"I'm just a little nervous about facing Freddy. I've built up meeting with him in my mind many times. Now it's time to truly tell him what I feel."

Cole reached out and rubbed her shoulder. "You'll be great. You're the bravest person I know. During this counseling, you've given me the strength to face monsters from my past, a strength I didn't think was possible. I want to thank you for that."

Maybe that was the reason he'd taken her out to the cabin—to thank her for helping him get over the loss of his brother. She and Cole had been through so much together in counseling, it wouldn't surprise her. And here for a moment she'd thought it might have to do with his feelings for *her*. She really was a dreamer, she told herself and turned to the window to gather her composure.

"Is that all you have to say?" Cole asked. "Where are you? What's going on inside that beautiful head of yours?"

"I never could stand that snake of a man, Freddy. But I couldn't say anything for Kendra's sake, so I took out my disgust on him one night when he tried to ask me out."

"What did you do to him?"

"He wasn't taking me seriously, so I kneed him where it hurts. After that, he got the point and stayed away." The memory brought a smile to her face.

"That weasel touched you?"

"He tried. I took care of him."

Cole gave a crooked smile. "Wish I could've been there to see you in action."

"Oh, it was beautiful. He yelped and fell to the ground. I told him to slither back to the hole he came from." Sashi felt more of her old self coming back just reliving the scene.

"That's a great story. Mind if I share it with the boys?" he asked.

"You can share it with anyone you want. It's really that good, huh?"

"It is."

Sashi felt a degree of pride. She needed to tap back into that person she used to be, a person who never let anything stop her. Today was a new beginning.

Cole pointed to a beautiful cove with four houses sitting along the water's edge. He motioned to a house up on a hill. "This is where the Powells all live, along with Sammi's grandparents, the Engstroms."

"How great that they all live so close together. They seemed like such a wonderful family."

"They're the best. We're going to be docking at CJ and Natasha's house. It's the one in the middle. Are you ready for a landing, Ms. Hansen?"

"Yes, Captain Stevens."

The landing was smooth with little wind to buffet the small plane. The sun was just beginning to set and the sky had started to come alive with the aurora borealis. Everywhere she looked, the landscape of this country seemed to draw her in like a moth to a flame. This place had a hold on her heart. She felt more at home here than Virginia. But this wasn't her life, and she needed to put such feelings away.

Cole jumped out of the plane and onto the state-of-the-art dock. He grabbed their bags and her crutches and placed them on the ground. Then he handed Sashi her crutches to help her get around.

Soon they heard people approaching. Sashi

looked up to see Jake, Sammi, Tasha, CJ, Doug, Doris and a handsome man who looked like Paul Bunyan coming down to greet them.

"Noah," Cole said to Paul Bunyan, "I didn't expect to see you here. It's been a while, buddy. I'd like to introduce you to Sashi Hansen. Sashi? This big boy right here is Noah Tanner, the skipper on one of the last two ranger boats serving the Tongass Forest."

"It's a pleasure to meet you, Noah." She smiled at him. "I'm curious about something. Do you all have a secret source of Treebeard's water? You know, from *The Lord of the Rings,* to make you all grow into giants?"

Her comment produced a round of laughter. Natasha and Sammi both told her they'd felt the same way when they came here.

"Cole, let's get Sashi inside and warm." Sashi appreciated Natasha's gentle suggestion. She *was* still healing after all.

"Of course," Jake replied. "Jeremiah, can you get her things?" They all made their way up to the immense red-planked home that stood partly over the water.

"Two questions for you, Cole," Sashi said. "Who is Jeremiah, and why is the house on stilts?"

"Jeremiah is CJ's middle name. It's a nickname now."

"Does he like it?"

"Yes. Ever since Tasha started calling him Jeremiah, it's been a keeper. And the house is on stilts to allow for the change in tides and tsunami waves."

"Oh. So why do Jake and Sammi live on the hill?"

"That's three questions."

"You." She nudged his shoulder.

Cole laughed. "Jake hates living too close to his parents, so he built his place higher up. Makes it difficult for his parents to come over all the time."

"But his house isn't *that* far away."

"I know. I've teased him about being a mama's boy for years."

Sashi couldn't help but chuckle. "What does he do?"

"He just teases me back."

"You two really are like brothers. Where did you guys meet?"

When Cole opened the door to the house, Sashi's jaw dropped. "Wow," she said.

"I know this place is a showpiece. Tasha doesn't talk about it, but she's a wealthy heiress from San Francisco."

"Wow again. She's so kind and friendly, you'd never guess. I've known a few people with money, and they make sure you know real fast who they are and how much they're worth."

"Not Tasha. Except for a few things like this house, she doesn't flaunt her money."

Sashi turned to Cole. "Kind of like you."

He looked shocked. "I don't have money. Just a doctor's salary."

"When you're ready to be honest one day, I'll be there to listen."

Cole took her on a tour of the house. It wasn't her taste, but it was stunning. Mahogany wood floors. A curved staircase going upstairs to open into a catwalk with rooms on both sides. A formal sitting area and piano on one side of the house. On the other, leather couches facing built-in cabinets with a huge TV screen.

When Cole helped her get comfortable on one of the burgundy-colored sofas, she said, "This must be your guys' domain."

"How did you guess?" He gave her a slow smile. His eyes roved over her, turning her insides to mush.

She needed to fight this absurd attraction. "So you never told me how you met Jake," she said.

There was a sound at the door and Jake walked in the room. "I can answer that for you. I met this turkey at Alaska University during our freshman year. We were both taking a paramedics course and he fell for me. What can I say? It was love at first sight."

Cole started to throw pillows at him. "I think it was the other way around, you clown. You needed me to help get you a date. You were so shy you couldn't even speak to girls."

"In your dreams, Stevens. We became roomies

all the way through grad school for me, and med school for pretty boy Cole."

"How did I put up with you and your fishy smell for so long, Powell?" Cole asked.

"I don't know what's worse. You came home smelling like formaldehyde or vomit depending on whether you were cutting up a corpse or dealing with sick patients."

"Boys, stop it!" Sammi interjected. She'd just come into the room. "I'm pregnant and this is making me feel ill."

Sashi laughed. "Are they always this bad?"

"Worse if they've been fishing and the fish are the same size. They measure the fish for days to see who caught the biggest. Always competitive. But they love each other like nothing else."

A huge dog came barreling in with a little girl clapping her hands behind him. "Do-gg."

"That's right, Christy. It's Beastly, your doggy."

"Do-gg, Mamaaa." Her big blue eyes shone with delight as she stared at her mom and patted Beastly's head.

Cole grinned at Sammi. "Until you came along, Christy, Beastly was the love of Jake's life. Everyone knows that."

Just then Doris, Jake and CJ's mom entered the room with coffee for everyone.

"Thank you," Sashi said.

"You're welcome," Doris replied. "I'm sure

you're exhausted. Those planes wear me out. The loud noise alone gives me a headache."

Sashi stared at the little girl and the dog. What a beautiful animal! She felt a tinge envious. She'd always wanted a dog, but her parents had always refused. How easy it was to imagine a life up here with Cole. To think of having a little boy or girl and a dog and friends who visited like this. It made her decision to leave Alaska that much harder.

"What kind of dog is he?" Sashi asked.

Jake replied jokingly, "*She's* a big old Rottweiler that Christy turned into a lap dog."

"Well, she's beautiful. You two are very blessed, especially with another baby on the way." Jake grabbed Sammi and pulled her onto his lap.

"I'm a lucky man. Don't know what I did to deserve it."

"Absolutely nothing," Cole threw out, which made Sashi laugh again.

"Uncle Cole, horsey?" said Christy. "Please?"

Sashi watched Cole drop to the floor on his hands and knees. He neighed like a horse. Christy toddled over and climbed onto his back with Cole's help. Soon the pair was circling the room. At last Cole stayed in one place and began to shake. "Bucking bronco!" he announced.

The little girl began laughing hysterically, and fearing she'd fall, Cole reached around for the little girl's body and extricated her from his back. He stood up and carried her to the couch.

"More, more!" Christy pleaded.

Cole turned around. "I'm sorry, cowgirl, that's enough for today. We'll go riding another day soon."

"Promise?"

"I promise." Cole crossed his heart with his fingers, then sat in a chair opposite Sashi.

Being in this house with Cole's friends and their families, seeing all the joy and the love, Sashi knew that this was what she wanted for herself. She really needed to get this confrontation with Freddy over with so she could return home soon.

As for Cole, when he looked at Sashi sitting so contentedly on the settee, he knew he was going to do all he could to keep her here in Alaska. He couldn't imagine his life without her in it.

Just then, Noah and CJ entered the room, along with Tasha. "I hate to break up the fun," Noah said, "but we need to leave if we're going to catch up with Trace and the rest of the group."

Cole stood up. "Are you ready to head out, Sashi? It will only take a day or so to catch up to the little SOB."

She nodded and placed her crutches at angles that would allow her to get up with ease. They headed out of the room and into the foyer, where Noah was talking to the others.

"We believe Freddy has been living in this area northwest of Marshall's," Noah said. "He's using very high-tech equipment to fish. Most of the smaller boats in the area can't afford that kind of thing. With the help from Jake using *his* high tech to track all the boats in the vicinity, we can identify who's using the deep sonar to fish. If Freddy's using it and we're close by, we'll surround him."

Cole turned to Sashi. "We're lucky Noah's going to help us. The *Chugach,* a ranger boat, will hold all of us. Freddy wouldn't expect it to come after him."

Doug came in. "Sounds like a plan," he said.

Noah gazed around. "Is everyone ready to go?"

Cole nodded. "Our stuff's in the plane. I'll grab it before we drive into Craig."

"Everything's in my truck," Jake said.

"My stuff's there, too." CJ echoed.

"Then let's head out." Noah nodded to the women and then to Doug and Doris Powell. "It's been a pleasure visiting with all of you. We'll be back as soon as possible." He headed out the door with a grace you wouldn't expect from such a tall man.

Sashi looked at Noah. If she weren't so in love with Cole, she might have been attracted to the handsome ranger. But Cole was a man a cut above the rest. His looks and brilliant mind made him the most intriguing man she'd ever met.

The group headed outside to jump into their cars. They'd head into the town of Craig where they would board the ranger boat. Sashi felt a thrill. She was finally going to face Freddy. No matter how it turned out, at least she would be following through on one of the promises she'd made to herself.

Doris had come outside with the group, and her eyes were tearing up. "I still don't understand why you all have to leap into the middle of danger," she said with a sniffle. "I love you all so much." She walked over and gave everyone a big hug. "Now come back safe."

"Ma," Jake said, "Freddy isn't a dangerous fugitive. He's a coward in hiding. We'll be fine. We just want to see him. Sashi has papers from the Knights to deliver to him, notifying him he was the father of Kendra's baby. She also needs to give that guy a good talking-to."

"Just the same, listen to your mother." Doug got into the act. "We love you."

Jake bent down and gave Christy a big hug and kiss. "Daddy has to go on a little trip for a day or so. I'll be home and bring you a present."

"Da-da." She smiled and gave him a wet kiss back. "Da-da." She clapped her hands again.

"Yes, Christy. You're very good at saying Daddy's name."

Sashi hoped that this enormous effort his friends were making was really going to work. She wondered how she was going to feel when she saw Freddy. In her heart she prayed the encounter would be constructive.

Chapter Nine

Sashi had drawn inward ever since they'd boarded the *Chugach*. She wanted to be careful in front of Cole's friends about their relationship. And as if in response, Cole, too, had become aloof, spending most of his time with the guys.

From her seat on the front deck of the boat, Sashi saw a land of unbelievable splendor. The intense blues and greens shimmering in the shoals on the rocky banks made her wish she'd brought a camera.

The Southwest Passage was a jewel left untouched by the rest of the world. The ship cut smoothly through the water, passing numerous small islands whose shores teemed with wildlife, sea lions barking as they lounged in the sun and bald eagles swooping down to perch in trees.

Yet Sashi had never felt so lonely. She needed to go home and see her parents, and there were a million things to do. This life of wonder with Cole could never be hers. Was it just wishful thinking that Cole was as in love with her as she was with him?

The *Chugach* began to slow, drawing Sashi's attention to another boat just off the starboard. As they drew closer she could see it was a larger, well-equipped fishing boat. Cole, CJ and Jake began to grab cables and ropes so they could connect the boats.

Would their skills ever cease to amaze her? She really was with the true outdoorsmen of the North and she continued to find herself loving it up here. If she had the freedom to love Cole, she couldn't imagine what a joy it would be to go on adventures with him when he had the time.

That dream needed to be put away. She needed to take care of her mental health or she wouldn't be good for anyone. The same with Cole. He still had issues. How could they have a true relationship until they'd become whole individuals themselves?

COLE WAS NERVOUS. THEY'D come upon Freddy's boat about five hours after they'd caught up with Trace, in a smaller fishing boat. The evening sky was darkening. He prayed Sashi would find the answers she was looking for.

Trace's boat pulled alongside the vessel Freddy had been living on for the past couple of months. Trace brought out a megaphone and began to speak.

"Freddy Marshall, this is Trace Hunter. I have a friend who needs to talk to you. If you refuse to speak to her, then we plan on blocking you into this area with a ranger boat till you give her a chance to speak."

There was silence before Cole saw Freddy appear along with his father, Frank. Frank used his megaphone. "Who wants to talk to us, Trace?"

The pounding in Cole's heart escalated as he watched the woman he loved stand up with her crutches and yell, "*I* do." She was so small, but so strong, he thought.

He could see Frank look at Sashi in surprise. "What do you want, Sashi? You have nothing to do with this."

Sashi swooped down on Trace. In a swift movement she grabbed the megaphone from his hand. In the process she dropped one of her crutches. "I want you to know I have *everything* to do with this. Do you know I was at the cabin that night, Frank? What about you, Freddy? Do you remember the terrible fight you had with Kendra? She told you she was pregnant with your child and you denied it? She was so upset she didn't know what to do, so she just ran. If you'd acknowledged that what she'd said was true, and you weren't so busy pawing Blake, she would still be alive. You son of a bitch, her death is your fault!"

Both of them looked taken back by her strong language. Freddy grabbed the megaphone from his dad. "I think that's unfair to put all this on me,

Sashi. I wasn't the father of her child. I didn't make her run into the forest."

Sashi dropped her other crutch as she leaned against the railing of the boat. "You're a liar!" Sashi reached into her pocket. "In my hand I have irrefutable evidence that you were the father. She was ten weeks along. How could you deny it? Who else did you think she was sleeping with? She was *in love* with you and you knew it, damn you. How could you have done that to her? Why did you lie and bring her all the way from the East Coast?"

Freddy was getting visibly agitated. His dad didn't look too pleased with him, either. "Sashi, my job is to bring women to the resort to work. The easiest way to get them was to let them believe I loved them. I *did* care for Kendra. But I wasn't ready to settle down. The idea of being a dad scared me. I've been hiding out and feeling terrible ever since I learned what had happened. I'm sorry, Sashi. So sorry for what you've been through."

He sounded sincere, Sashi thought, then felt an arm slip around her waist. Cole. His touch gave her the strength to continue. "I believe you, Freddy. And I accept your apology. But you still need to talk to Kendra's parents, the Knights. They deserve to hear the truth from you personally." She took a deep breath. "And you, Frank Marshall, you need to treat your employees better. We're not slaves, we're humans who have rights. Start thinking about it before you're faced with a class action suit from all your employees, past and present."

Sashi handed the megaphone back to Trace. "Thank you," she murmured. "I feel much better."

COLE GRABBED HER CRUTCHES and helped her into the cabin, where he placed a blanket around her shoulders and made her sit.

"You did an amazing job, Sashi. You really humbled that SOB."

"Thanks. I feel so much better. It's going to take time to get *all* my anger out, but I feel as if I've done a lot to purge myself of those terrible feelings. I also feel I'll be able to return home soon."

Cole felt as if he'd been hit with a ton of bricks. There had to be a way he could convince her to stay. "Sashi," he said, "will you come with me and help me let go of some of *my* pain?"

"All right. Where are we going?"

"Let me surprise you."

THE FLIGHT TO VALDEZ took the rest of day. They made gas stops along the way. Sashi couldn't remember being this happy in months, not since well before the attack. She was happy that Cole wanted her to help him get over some of his fears.

She wondered if helping him would draw them closer. Could they fight their way to each other? Only time would tell. Today she was excited to see what would happen next. No feelings of impending doom.

Looking out the windows, she saw the biggest mountains she'd ever seen in her life. They rose like centurions from the crystal-blue sea, jutting up thousands and thousands of feet in the air. Valdez was nestled in the foothills and on the shoreline.

Sashi turned to Cole. "Why did you ever leave this place? It's stunning."

Cole glanced at her. "It'll always be home, but I've built my life in Tongass. And it snows here too much for me."

"That's right. You used to be a world-class skier. Do you still ski?"

"Yes, but not like I used to. I didn't push myself hard enough with rehab. Instead I turned to my studies. I didn't want to be reminded of Luke all the time. It's my own fault. Don't get me wrong. I've rehabbed my body now, but lost the edge I had when I was younger. I hope you won't do what I did."

"I don't plan on it. All of you—Mary, Dr. Samuelson—have given me such inspiration, I don't want to give up on my dream. I love to dance too much."

"I'm glad to hear that. You're an amazing woman." He leaned over and kissed her cheek.

The gesture surprised and moved her. She knew she was healing. The one area she still needed to work on was forgiving herself. Hopefully she would find a way to do that.

They landed at a private airport, where they were greeted by an attendant. The door to the cockpit opened. "Welcome, Dr. Stevens. Your parents are thrilled to have you home, sir. They're also excited to meet Ms. Hansen."

"Thanks, Jens."

Five minutes later they were loaded into an enormous Cadillac Escalade. Jens was the driver.

Sashi stared at Cole. "I seem to recall a little conversation about how you were just a doctor who lived on his salary."

Cole leaned back in the seat and drew her into his arms as close as he could with the seat belts restraining them. "Can we talk about it later?" There were a million reasons for her to fight having Cole hold her so close. Yet there was something about this setting, and Cole's response to her. He was completely attuned to everything she was doing. It was also comforting to have Cole hold her in his arms for a while—it had been a hellish twenty-four hours.

"Sure."

"How did you figure it out, anyway?" Cole wanted to know.

"The way you live—your house—the way you talked about the arts. There's an air about you, but I didn't guess it the first time I met you. Over time it started to make sense."

"Good. I don't like people to know."

Cole kissed her hair, then relaxed. The poor man must be exhausted. She realized after a moment that he'd dozed off with her in his arms.

What a wonderful feeling! She didn't know how her luck had turned the way it had, but she was so grateful Cole had been the one to find her.

She relished this moment, though she was nervous about meeting his parents. What if they didn't like her? She wondered if he'd brought many women home before. What other things did he want to do up here at his parents' house?

Sashi had a lot of questions, but she realized she needed to stop worrying and just let life happen. He said he needed her help and she wanted to help him any way she could. Cole had done nothing but help *her* since the bear attack. It was nice to be needed for once.

The car was heading up into the hills now. As they climbed higher, the homes became mansions in the style of ski lodges. Some were like places she'd seen in photos of the Swiss Alps. Others were more contemporary with big wooden beams and peaked roofs like Marshall's. When she'd realized Cole came from money, she truly had no idea what kind of money.

Jens slowed and made a stop at a gate with a coded entrance. She was surprised how much snow had already fallen up here—it was mid-October. She could see that if you didn't love snow, you wouldn't want to live here. But to her it was all so beautiful.

They drove up a paved driveway that was snow-free. The upkeep had to be staggering, she thought. Once they rounded a corner, a home came into view that looked like it belonged in a European village. It was charming, yet immense with a stone chimney and stenciled flowers all over the exterior. There was even a medieval-style turret in the middle of the home.

Sashi rubbed her cheek against Cole's slightly bristled one. "I think we've arrived."

Cole's eyes opened, and he leaned over and gave her a quick kiss on the lips. Then he sat up and looked around. "Yup. This is their place."

"It's pretty incredible," she said in a quiet voice.

"It's home. Let's go inside. I'm dying for a shower." His eyes traveled over her body taking in the cream camisole and sweater set she wore to match with a pair of navy slacks. She'd taken off her jacket. Cole traced his finger along the top edge of her camisole. "You look stunning today, New York. I can't wait to get you alone."

His touch and words made her mind go hazy. The idea of being seduced by Cole had been something she hadn't allowed herself to think about since she'd been attacked. Now that the idea was a possibility, her body was on fire and all she wanted to do was respond.

Was this what he needed help with? No. She

knew there was something else. But his loving re-
sponses to her were breaking down barriers she'd
fought to keep up. It was rattling all of her senses.

There was a knock on the car door, then it
opened to Jens.

"I'll have your luggage brought up to your
rooms," he said. "Your parents are waiting for you
in the salon."

"Thanks, Jens." Cole got out of the car, then
eyed Sashi one more time before he handed her the
crutches. Sashi was becoming a master of getting
out of cars, and she thumped her way into a home
unlike any she'd ever seen before. The decor was
stunning, from the marble-tiled floors to the paintings on the walls, to the arched ceiling.

Cole led her through the home to a cozy room—
the salon—with a fireplace decorated with hunting gear and trophy heads of various animals. The
furniture was modern—puffy leather couches and
a TV built into the wall. Obviously a family room.

The couple sitting on one of the couches got to
their feet. Attractive and smiling, they were obviously Cole's parents. Cole put his arm around her
shoulder so he could massage the back of her neck.
Did he have any idea that his touch made it difficult to pay attention to what others were saying?

His father had the same steady gaze along with
the same height and build. He'd gone gray, but was
handsome with a friendly smile and deep dimples.
His mother was beautiful. She still had the same

color of blond hair as Cole, as well as his sensational eyes. The genes didn't lie. His mother was a slender woman of medium height who seemed absolutely thrilled to see her son.

"Cole, darling!" she spoke first. "What have you gotten yourself into again? Do you know how much we worry about you?" With tears in her eyes she reached out and hugged him tightly.

Then his dad reached out and hugged him. "Cole, we've been waiting for you. I've missed my boy. How are you?"

Sashi could see the dynamic in play here. His parents had never blamed him for Luke's death. Only Cole did, and he had yet to forgive himself. That was why he'd stayed away.

Cole drew Sashi forward and looped an arm across her shoulders. "Mom and Dad, I'd like you to meet Sashi Hansen. Sashi? My parents, Richard and Lucy Stevens."

"It's a pleasure to meet both of you, as well." She freed her right hand from her crutches and held it out. Both Richard and Lucy grasped it warmly. "I can't tell you what a blessing it has been for me to meet Cole," Sashi said. "He saved my life." Her eyes misted over.

Richard and then Lucy gave her a big hug. "That's what he does, my dear," Lucy said with a wink. "But you're the first woman our Cole has ever brought home."

Richard nodded. "We're excited to meet you and

get to know you. We'd love to hear this story if you feel comfortable talking about it."

Sashi nodded. "I'm happy to."

"Mom and Dad, give the poor girl room to breathe. She can tell you the story tonight at dinner."

Richard jumped back in. "We understand you're a dancer who studied in New York. It's hard to believe that a woman as beautiful and talented as you came into Cole's life out here in the wilds of Alaska, and we're dying to hear—"

Cole put his hand up. "Sashi is still recovering from some serious injuries. She needs to rest and I really need a shower. Can we talk about all this at dinner?"

"Of course," Lucy said. "But at dinner, you two are fair game."

Sashi started to laugh. "You can ask away, Mrs. Stevens."

"Oh, no, please call me Lucy. Now let's get you to your rooms. Cole said you both have your own room? Correct?"

Sashi nodded. She could tell Lucy was trying to figure out the nature of their relationship. Her guess was as good as Sashi's. It was too complicated to think about right now. A shower and a nap sounded good.

"I'll show you to your rooms."

AFTER A SUMPTUOUS MEAL of rack of lamb with rosemary potatoes and a mixed green salad, Cole, Sashi and his parents relaxed in the family room. Cole sat with Sashi in the crook of his arm, facing his parents. The home had outdoor lighting, and they could see the snow falling outside.

For the first time since Luke had died, Cole felt peaceful being in this cozy atmosphere. "Mom and Dad, I need to talk to you."

His father looked at him with love. "We're all ears, Cole."

Cole closed his eyes and took a deep breath. His hand shook as he drew a letter from his pocket. He'd written it while he'd been sitting on the boat looking for Freddy.

He gently removed his arm from around Sashi and leaned forward. He looked his mother, then his father in the eye. "First, I want you to know that Sashi is very important to me."

Lucy smiled. "For you to bring her home, we assume she must be."

Cole's eyes suddenly brimmed with tears. "Sashi has helped me more than anyone could ever know. She thinks I saved *her* when she was injured some weeks ago, but really, she has saved *me*." Cole glanced at Sashi, saw her confusion.

"I want to read you a letter I've written to Luke."

He could hear his mother's sharp intake of breath. "What is this about, sweetheart?" she asked.

"I'm finally in a place where I can forgive myself for Luke's death. And I hope *you* can forgive me for letting him die on that mountain." Cole's heart was pounding as he said the words, but with Sashi at his side, he had the courage to forgive himself and ask for his parents' forgiveness, too."

He stood up when he saw his parents get up from the sofa they'd been sitting on. Their eyes filled with tears, they crossed the room to embrace him. "Son, we never held you responsible," Richard said. "Not ever. Where did you get that idea?"

"I blamed myself, so I believed you blamed me, too," Cole responded.

"Oh, darling—" Lucy cupped his face in her hands "—how did we not see this before now? You're our precious boy. We love you and were so grateful that you lived. Maybe we got so caught up in mourning, we didn't see your pain. Will you forgive us for not knowing?"

She hugged him close. "What a terrible burden you've carried all these years. We never ever blamed you, Cole. It was a terrible accident."

Sashi sat on the couch as a bystander, tears of joy and pain streaming down her cheeks. How wonderful for Cole to finally be rid of the burden. She was happy for him, although she felt awkward being present at such a private family moment.

But then Lucy turned to her. "Thank you for bringing our son back to us, Sashi." Lucy bent down and hugged her. "Thank you for your strength."

Richard came over and kissed her on the cheek. "You're both strong," he said. "You've given us a gift that is irreplaceable." He sat down by Cole, who resumed his position on the couch with Sashi.

Lucy sat on the ottoman right in front of Sashi and Cole. "I want you to save that letter, Cole, and tell it to Luke. It's private. Whatever is in it is between you and him. We've let go of Luke years ago and moved on. He still lives in our hearts, but it doesn't hurt so much anymore. We want the same for you."

Sashi looked at Cole and could see a light in his tawny eyes. She didn't think he'd ever looked more beautiful than he did now. He seemed completely happy and at rest.

Cole focused on her, and she could see the love in his eyes. "Sashi, will you come up in a helicopter with me tomorrow so I can read my letter to Luke at the place where he died, then shred it and throw it to the wind?"

The thought of being in a helicopter made her a little nervous. But she knew she'd do anything to help Cole heal. "Of course," she said.

Chapter Ten

It was a beautiful sunny morning in the back country of the Chugach Mountains. Jagged, snow-packed peaks soaring to heights of thirteen thousand feet surrounded them. The small, piloted helicopter Cole had hired carried them around chutes and crannies of the rugged terrain to their final destination.

Sashi wore a parka that Cole's mom had lent her. It was a little big, but it was warm and that was all that mattered. She tapped Cole's shoulder and yelled, "I can't believe you jumped out of a helicopter and skied up here!"

His face lit up. "I *still* do it."

Sashi shook her head. "No, you don't. I don't think I could handle that." Her heart skittered all over the place. But then she realized he didn't belong to her, nor she to him.

"How about this—we'll talk about it," he responded.

The helicopter now hovered above a huge chute.

"Is this where you and Luke jumped?" It didn't look humanly possible to even stay on the slope, let alone ski down it.

"Yes!" He nodded. "Come closer so you can hear me. I want you to know what the letter says."

"Okay."

Cole leaned over to help her get unbuckled and put her on his lap.

The pilot of the helicopter gave Cole a three-minute warning signal with his hand. Cole gave him a thumbs-up, pulled out the letter and began to read.

Luke,

It's been twenty years since I've been able to talk to you. You were the best big brother a guy could ever have. I now realize you wouldn't have wanted me to blame myself for your death.

But I'm still so sorry for what happened. There isn't a day that goes by that I don't miss you. I just want you to know I'm going to start living my life now.

Thank you for showing your little brother all the love you did. You were the best at everything and I've tried to live up to your standards. I'll always keep your memory alive in my heart. I love you.

COLE PUT SASHI DOWN ON her seat then began to tear up the letter. He moved to the door of the helicopter, opened it and threw the bits of papers to the wind. The relief and weight that vanished with the papers was obvious. He looked like a new man.

The arctic air that filled the belly of the helicopter was like a slap in the face for Sashi. She could see what forgiveness had done for Cole. Now it was *her* turn. She really needed to heal on the inside before she could be in a serious relationship with anyone.

Cole closed the door and sat back down in the seat next to her.

"Ready for some lunch?" he asked.

She nodded.

COLE HAD GONE TO WORK that afternoon decorating the family's yacht moored to the docks, into a floating palace of lights. He'd wanted everything to be perfect tonight when he proposed to Sashi. He'd even called her parents today.

They had given their consent if it was what Sashi wanted. Everything was falling into place. Ridding himself of that burden had changed his outlook. He was a different man. He had found the perfect woman and he was not going to let her get away.

He'd left Sashi some money so she could buy a dress in town for their special date tonight. With Jens as her driver, he knew she would be well taken care of.

More than anything he couldn't wait to see his diamond on her finger. Cole patted the breast pocket of his jacket, double-checking to make sure it was there. He and his dad had bought a ring today at the jeweler's. Now it sat in his pocket all ready to be placed on her finger. All he could do was hope that she would like the ring and love the man who wanted to give it to her.

The phone in his pocket rang. "Dr. Stevens," he said.

"This is Jens, sir. We've arrived. Would you like me to escort Miss Hansen in? Or would you like to come and get her?"

"I'll be right out. And, Jens, thanks for your help today."

"You're most welcome, sir."

SASHI SAT IN THE BACK of the Cadillac Escalade wondering what was going to happen. When Cole had told her to buy a special dress for the evening, she thought it meant a dinner with his parents. Clearly that wasn't the case since she'd said goodbye to them earlier at the house.

Now why was Jens pulling into the harbor? Then she saw the beautiful yacht tethered to the dock. It was festooned with colorful lights and looked... enchanted.

Tonight she was grateful she hadn't spent all the money he'd given her on the outfit she was wearing—he had already done too much. Especially when she saw the price tags at the boutique Jens had taken her to at first. She'd cringed inwardly, then clunked out the door on her crutches. Once outside she'd asked Jens if he knew of any second-hand stores.

He did, and at one of them she found the perfect dress—a sleeveless black silk that hugged her body perfectly, falling just above her knees. The store had a pair of black kitten heels to match the gown, allowing her to walk steadily with crutches. To finish off the look, she pulled her hair up into a loose chignon, leaving tendrils of hair to frame her face.

She watched as Cole exited the yacht and walked to the Cadillac. He looked incredibly sexy in a perfectly tailored suit. He opened her door and leaned in. His eyes swept over her. "Do you want to walk with your crutches or do you want me to carry you?"

The way he looked, smiled and the exhilarating smell of his aftershave titillated her senses. But she'd vowed to be strong and not rely on him for everything. "I think I can manage on my own."

He helped her out of the Cadillac, then reached in for her crutches, which he handed to her. The wind off the water was bone chilling, and Sashi shivered, despite the long cashmere coat Cole's mom had lent her.

Jens drove off as she and Cole walked together onto the dock and onto the yacht. Sashi had seen boats like this in films, but never in real life. "This is beautiful, Cole!" she breathed.

"I'm glad you like it."

"Who wouldn't? It's incredible, and the lights…" She was speechless as he ushered her inside.

Cole moved in closer to her, making her yearn for something she knew she couldn't have. He deserved someone better than her, a woman who wasn't broken. Before Cole found forgiveness, they were two lost souls who clung to one another for help and security.

He helped her off with her coat, then brought his hands up to cup her face. "Sashi, you're so damn beautiful." Then his hands slid down to her waist and he pulled her close.

She leaned back slightly to meet his gaze, and she couldn't recall a time she'd ever seen so much desire. When he lowered his head and their lips met, her resolve to keep her distance melted away. The kiss was hot and wet, and seemed to go on and on. Sashi ran her hands through his hair and started to remove his jacket. One of his hands began to unzip her dress.

The sound brought her out of her sensual trance. "Cole, we need to…" But no words could come out. The aurora borealis was out tonight in its full grandeur. The sky kept flashing a green light over the mountains and bay, creating an atmosphere of supreme brilliance from the snow-covered peaks to the ocean below.

"No words could do justice to the beauty of this night sky. I could only imagine creating a dance to show the splendor of what I have seen tonight.

Too bad I don't have a camera and can't take pictures very well."

"Sammi is a professional photographer. I'm sure she has hundreds of pictures you could choose from of the aurora borealis."

She bumped into his shoulder. "Thanks. I have a question though."

"You have a question?"

"Yes. Are we going to have dinner tonight?"

He looked a bit stunned. "Uh, it's all ready for us to eat."

COLE DIDN'T KNOW WHAT to make of this new woman. He had never seen her like this before. All through dinner she was fun, sweet and loving, but something had changed since this afternoon. He could feel she was holding herself back. Maybe when he proposed, it would allay all her fears.

The red and white roses all over the countertops and the lit candles created an atmosphere of romance. He stood up and crossed to the sound system, then put on the song they had danced to so many weeks ago in his room. "I've come to think of this as our song. Would you dance with me again, Sashi?"

"As long as you help, Doc."

Doc? He winced. Where was all this friend stuff coming from?

Sashi stood on her own, waiting for Cole to come. She'd taken her shoes off in anticipation before he reached her. When he did, Sashi put her good foot on his right foot, and seconds later, they began to move to the rhythm. To Cole it was heaven.

Once the song ended, Cole got down on one knee and pulled out the little box containing the ring. "Sashi Hansen," he began, "I love you. Will you marry me and live with me here in Alaska?"

SASHI WAS BLOWN AWAY. She knew that Cole had feelings for her. But she hadn't anticipated a marriage proposal so soon. Cole must have had an epiphany in the helicopter that morning.

Between finding forgiveness from his parents and writing the letter to Luke, he'd obviously found the peace *she* was so desperately looking for. His guilty feelings must have gone to the wind right along with the pieces of paper.

She, however, couldn't say yes until she'd reached the same level of self-forgiveness as Cole. It wouldn't be fair to him. She would be cheating him out of the life he deserved.

The ring was so beautiful she could barely take her eyes off it. It was at least a carat and a half emerald-cut diamond with two emeralds on either side half the size in the same shape. And Cole was hoping to slide it on her finger.

"Cole," she began, "the ring is absolutely gorgeous. But I can't say yes right now. I don't know if I'll ever be ready for a real relationship. I'm so sorry. Today when I saw you forgive yourself over your brother's death, I realized I still needed time to heal. You deserve a woman who can give herself wholeheartedly to you. But I'm still stuck and I refuse to drag you back to that dark place."

"Sashi, I can help you. You helped me. We can do this together. We can make it work!"

"I can't. Until I can fill this void in my soul, I'm no good for anyone. I'm so sorry, Cole. I never meant to hurt you."

Sashi's heart was breaking as she watched him close the tiny box. "I have major obstacles to overcome. I have to forgive myself, and I have to make things right with Kendra's parents. Until I heal, I can't be the strong person you need.

"I also need to see my parents. I miss them. It's a huge decision for me to leave everything I've ever known and live in Alaska. And I don't know that there will be children here who'll want to take dance classes."

"There will always be room in Alaska for a dance teacher," he said. "But it was foolish and selfish of me to ask you to marry me and live here. I'm sorry to have put pressure on you—I know better than anyone what you're going through. Forgive me, Sashi. I'll let you go to find the peace you deserve."

Sashi's lower lip began to tremble. "It's also hard for me to imagine a life without you." She started to cry.

Cole took her in his arms and held her for long minutes, then let her go. She watched a curtain fall over his face.

"Can you please take me back to your parents' home?" she asked.

"Sure. Let's go." He blew out the candles, turned off the lights and handed Sashi her crutches, then headed to the deck above. Sashi's tears slipped down her cheeks as she climbed the stairs with the help of the railing.

I've done it now, she thought. *I've truly lost any chance to be with Cole.*

WHEN THEY RETURNED TO KETCHIKAN, Sashi found that her parents and the Knights had arrived and were staying at a hotel in town. Mary, it seemed, had called them and told them Sashi was much better, and they had all come to accompany her on her flight back to Virginia.

Sashi learned that the Knights had flown to Prince of Wales Island to visit Frank Marshall and Freddy at the resort. Apparently they'd given the Marshalls hell for what had happened.

Sashi asked Mrs. Knight, "Do you feel better?"

"Talking to that young man will never bring my Kendra back," Mrs. Knight said, "but it felt good to give him a piece of my mind."

Sashi decided that after what she'd done to Cole, it would be best for her to take a room at the same hotel as her parents.

IT WAS SASHI'S LAST NIGHT in Alaska. Doris had called and invited the group to her home for a good-bye dinner. Sashi was nervous and excited to see Cole after almost a week—a week that had been one of the worst she'd had up here. She had to find a way to get over Cole, or she was going to be miserable for the rest of her life.

To her dismay, Cole wasn't there. She shouldn't be surprised, not after the way they'd parted. But the house was filled with well-wishers from the hospital and all of Cole's friends. She loved seeing Doris, Doug, Sammi, Jake, CJ and Natasha, Nels and his wife, Marta. She hated having to say goodbye.

She'd be eternally grateful for all their support. She'd never anticipated finding a warm surrogate family in the cold North. In a strange way, though, it hurt to look at them, knowing they all loved Cole and probably didn't understand why she was leaving him. She only knew that it was the right thing to do.

The feast on the dining room table was dazzling. Clam chowder, fresh crusty bread, shrimp, crab, rice pilaf and various salads. But Sashi found she could eat very little. Her appetite for food had disappeared. She realized she needed to talk to Kendra's parents now, before they all flew out tomorrow.

As she approached them, she could feel her heart pounding and her head starting to ache. But this was something she was not going to back down from.

"Mr. and Mrs. Knight, could I talk to you privately? Just for a moment."

"Of course, darling," Mrs. Knight replied.

They followed her into a small den. The Knights sat on a small leather couch and Sashi sat in a chair facing them. Then she took a deep breath and began. "I can't even begin to tell you how sorry I am for letting Kendra die—even though it was Freddy's actions that made her run outside. I hope you know I loved her like a sister."

Walt reached over and took Sashi's hand in his. "Sashi, we have known you since you were three and riding around on your tricycle. You brought nothing but joy to Kendra. To all of us." He glanced at his wife, who nodded vigorously.

Sashi could feel her eyes begin to tear up.

"You didn't 'let' her get killed," he went on. "We heard that you threw yourself in front of a bear to save our daughter's life. What an incredible act of bravery and…" He seemed to choke up, and he looked down at the floor and coughed. Then he brought a hand up to cover his mouth and started to cry.

His wife jumped in, rubbing her husband's back. "We have wanted to thank you for so long now. What you did took not only bravery, but love. Love for our daughter. What a wonderful friend you were. We love you very much."

The Knights both reached over and tugged her gently to come sit between them on the couch. Soon all three were hugging and crying. Sashi realized that she had finally gotten to the point where she could forgive herself.

A huge weight was lifted from her shoulders.

Now she needed to go find Cole and make things right with him—if he still wanted her.

She sought out Jake. If anybody knew where Cole was, it would be his best friend.

AT THE AGE OF FIFTEEN, when Cole had lost his older brother, he thought he knew heartbreak. But losing the woman you love was equally heartbreaking. Cole had tried all week to throw himself into his work, but it couldn't take his mind off of Sashi.

He thought about taking a tropical vacation. But going somewhere romantic without Sashi sounded like another type of torture.

Coming out here again to Humpback Lake was the best thing he could have done for himself. He still couldn't understand why Sashi had turned him down flat. But the wilderness was a great place to be alone and think, while indulging in his favorite pastimes—hiking, fishing and hunting.

Today's hike lifted his spirits a little. Now he could do a little fishing. He jumped across the waterfall and headed into the cabin.

The sight that met his eyes left him momentarily speechless. Sashi was sitting at the picnic

table wearing a fitted long-sleeve shirt and jeans.
Her glorious hair was down. And the cabin had
been transformed from his den of disaster into a
romantic retreat.

Cole thought he could devour her right there
on the table. But he needed to know why she was
out here?

Candles flickered on every surface. The picnic table was covered with a white tablecloth.
There was a spread of food on it similar to the
one he'd supplied when he'd brought her out to
the lake.

His appetite, however, was more for her than the
food. He was angry at himself for still wanting her.
And then angry at *her* for toying with his this way.

"Sashi, what are you doing here?"

She rose from the table, using a cane to stabi-
lize herself. "I came to find you and talk to you."

"I think you've already said enough."

"No, you need to hear what I have to say. And I
need you to hear it." Her voice was shaking.

He sighed and said curtly, "Hurry up, then I'll
fly you home."

He could see the flash of pain in her eyes. But
he couldn't handle being around this woman who'd
rejected him for any length of time.

"I had an amazing talk with the Knights," she
said. "I asked them to forgive me. Not only did they
forgive me, but they told me they loved me and
were grateful I'd stood up to the bear like I did."

"And what does this have to do with me?"

"Everything! When I heard their utter forgiveness, it took me by complete surprise. Their love and acceptance have helped me to forgive myself, take away the pain I've been carrying around over Kendra. I finally realized it wasn't my fault.

"It wasn't anyone's fault. It was just something terrible that happened. A whim of fate. I've also let go of my anger against Freddy. I feel like I've exorcised these bad feelings from my soul and am ready to start a new life with you. If you'll give me another chance, that is."

He stared at her, his heart pounding. Was she really saying…?

She moved closer to him, then lifted her head and looked him directly in the eye. "Cole, I want to know if your offer still stands."

"What offer?" he asked, still in a state of disbelief.

"Your offer of marriage."

He watched a smile spread across her beautiful face. He waited a beat, then said, "Hold on. Let me get something." Cole went rummaging through his duffel bags and came out with the tiny black jeweler's box.

He heard her gasp, then he got down on one knee in front of her. "Sashi Hansen, will you make me the happiest man in the—"

"Yes, yes, yes!" she cried.

"Well, New York, I always wanted to propose to you in this cabin and now I've got my wish."

He slipped the ring on her finger, then folded her in his arms.

* * * * *

COMING NEXT MONTH
from Harlequin® American Romance®

AVAILABLE MARCH 5, 2013

#1441 COWBOY FOR KEEPS
Mustang Valley
Cathy McDavid

Conner Durham can't believe his luck—Dallas Sorrenson is finally single and free to date. Then he learns she's pregnant...and the father is the man who stole Conner's job.

#1442 BETTING ON TEXAS
Amanda Renee

City girl Miranda Archer buys a ranch in Texas, hoping to start over. But she has apparently stolen it from Jesse Langtry—a cowboy who's rugged, gorgeous and madder than hell at her!

#1443 THE BABY JACKPOT
Safe Harbor Medical
Jacqueline Diamond

After an unexpected night with sexy surgeon Cole Rattigan, nurse Stacy Layne discovers she's pregnant. But her recent donation of eggs to a childless couple means her hormones have gone wild. Result: she's carrying triplets!

#1444 A NANNY FOR THE COWBOY
Fatherhood
Roxann Delaney

Luke Walker desperately needs a nanny for his young son. Hayley Brooks needs a job. It's a perfect match—in more ways than one!

HARCNM0213

REQUEST YOUR FREE BOOKS!
2 FREE NOVELS PLUS 2 FREE GIFTS!

HARLEQUIN®

American ★ Romance®

LOVE, HOME & HAPPINESS

Welcome back to MUSTANG VALLEY,
and Cathy McDavid's final book in this series.
Conner Durham has gone from flashy executive to simple
cowboy seemingly overnight. At least Dallas Sorrenson
has appeared back in his life—and she's
apparently single!

The laughter, light and musical, struck a too-familiar chord. His steps faltered, and then stopped altogether. It couldn't be her! He must be mistaken.

Conner's hands involuntarily clenched. Gavin wouldn't blindside him like this. He'd assured Conner weeks ago that Dallas Sorrenson had declined their request to work on the book about Prince due to a schedule conflict. Her wedding, Conner had assumed.

And, yet, there was no mistaking that laughter, which drifted again through the closed office door.

With an arm that suddenly weighed a hundred pounds, he grasped the knob, pushed the door open and entered the office.

Dallas turned immediately and greeted him with a huge smile. The kind of bright, sexy smile that had most men— Conner included—angling for the chance to get near her.

Except, she was married, or soon to be married. He couldn't remember the date.

And her husband, or husband-to-be, was Conner's former coworker and pal. The man whose life remained perfect while Conner's took a nosedive.

"It's so good to see you again!" Dallas came toward him.

He reached out his hand to shake hers. "Hey, Dallas."

With an easy grace, she ignored his hand and wound her arms loosely around his neck for a friendly hug. Against his better judgment, Conner folded her in his embrace and drew her close. She smelled like spring flowers and felt like every man's fantasy. Then again, she always had.

"How have you been?"

Rather than state the obvious, that he was still looking for a job and just managing to survive, he answered, "Fine. How 'bout yourself?"

"Great."

She looked as happy as she sounded. Married life obviously agreed with her. "And how is Richard?"

"Actually, I wouldn't know." An indefinable emotion flickered in her eyes. "As of two months ago, we're no longer engaged."

It took several seconds for her words to register; longer for their implication to sink in.

Dallas Sorrenson was not just single, she was available.

Look for COWBOY FOR KEEPS, coming this March 2013 only from Harlequin American Romance!

There's more than a ranch at stake for this cowboy....

When Miranda Archer bought Double Trouble Ranch, sight unseen, she was eager to leave city life behind and start fresh in the Texas Hill Country. But the property came with some unexpected extras: a few cattle, a couple of horses…and one surly cowboy.

Sure that rural life will be too much for Miranda, Jesse Langtry bets her that she won't last a month at Double Trouble. If he wins, she'll sell him the land—if *she* wins, he'll leave for good. Pushing each other away seems to bring them closer—and that's where the real trouble begins!

Betting on Texas

by AMANDA RENEE

**Available from Harlequin® American Romance®
March 5, 2013!**

They Know Everything About Babies....

So why is recently single Stacy Layne suddenly on the mommy fast track? As Safe Harbor Medical's first successful egg donor, she should have known better. That goes double—or should she say *triple?*—for Cole Rattigan, the country's leading fertility surgeon.

Cole prefers the operating room to figuring out what's going on inside a woman's head. But after an unplanned night of passion with his favorite nurse, the man who wrote the book on fertility is about to become a father... three times over!

Can a man who's just discovering his paternal side find the words to let the woman he loves know how much he cares?

Find out in

The Baby Jackpot

by JACQUELINE DIAMOND

**Available from Harlequin® American Romance®
March 5, 2013!**

HARLEQUIN®

A *Romance* FOR EVERY MOOD™

**Stay up-to-date on all your
romance-reading news with the
Harlequin Shopping Guide,
featuring bestselling authors, exciting new
miniseries, books to watch and more!**

The newest issue will be delivered right to you
with our compliments! There are 4 each year.

Signing up is easy.

EMAIL

ShoppingGuide@Harlequin.ca

WRITE TO US

HARLEQUIN BOOKS
Attention: Customer Service Department
P.O. Box 9057, Buffalo, NY 14269-9057

OR PHONE

1-800-873-8635 in the United States
1-888-343-9777 in Canada

Please allow 4-6 weeks for delivery of the first issue by mail.

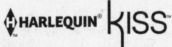